James Rindge Stanwood

The Direct Ancestry of the late Jacob Wendell, of

Portsmouth, New Hampshire

with a prefatory sketch of the early Dutch settlement of the province of

New Netherland, 1614-1664

James Rindge Stanwood

The Direct Ancestry of the late Jacob Wendell, of Portsmouth, New Hampshire
with a prefatory sketch of the early Dutch settlement of the province of New Netherland, 1614-1664

ISBN/EAN: 9783337302245

Printed in Europe, USA, Canada, Australia, Japan

Cover: Foto ©Andreas Hilbeck / pixelio.de

More available books at **www.hansebooks.com**

THE

DIRECT ANCESTRY

OF

THE LATE JACOB WENDELL,

OF PORTSMOUTH, NEW HAMPSHIRE,

WITH A

Prefatory Sketch

OF THE

EARLY DUTCH SETTLEMENT

OF THE

PROVINCE OF NEW NETHERLAND.

1614—1664.

BY

JAMES RINDGE STANWOOD,

OF BOSTON.

BOSTON:
SPECIAL LIMITED EDITION.
DAVID CLAPP & SON.
1882.

TABLE OF CONTENTS.

No. 1.

PREFACE.

In the introductory sketch of the period included within the years 1614–1664, it has been essayed briefly to portray the sway of the United Provinces over New Netherland, the limits of which originally extended from Chesapeake Bay to Cape Cod, but were subsequently greatly modified. At the end of that time, embracing a period of half a century, the influence of England had become preponderant in America, and the rapidly growing commercial importance of the valuable territory held by the Dutch did not escape the notice of that power. The English Crown, under cover of enforcing the Navigation Law of 1663, resolved to add the coveted region to its dominion, and the following year Charles and his ministers seized the province, the present site of three great states of the American Union.

In presenting the genealogical data contained within these pages, the author desires to state that this little volume does not purport to follow the history of the various branches of a name whose ramifications are both numerous and extensive. It is designed simply to condense in a convenient hand-book for genealogical reference, the record of the direct ancestry of the late Jacob Wendell, of Portsmouth, New Hampshire. That gentleman, the author's grandfather, of revered memory, deceased August 27, 1865. He was descended in the sixth generation, through JOHANNES, 1649, from EVERT JANSEN WENDEL, of Albany—the First Settler of the name, who came to America in 1640—by his first wife, Susanna Du Trieux.

The descendant of any of those early families who settled along the banks of the Hudson under the gentle rule of Holland, recurring with honest pride to more than two centuries of honorable lineage, realizes his indebtedness to past generations. And as he searches their annals, inscribed in quaint Netherland-Dutch, in the very curious and interesting Notarial Papers, he adequately appreciates the services rendered to his kinsmen by Professor Jonathan Pearson, of Union College. The laborious and studious researches of this gentleman among the Dutch manuscripts at Albany, and the result of years of patient investigation, are exhibited in his valuable contributions for the genealogies of the First Settlers of that ancient borough. Of the material aid furnished by these the author has gladly availed himself, and additionally of the courtesy of Professor Pearson, who has kindly allowed the proof-sheets of this pamphlet to receive his examination and approval.

JAMES RINDGE STANWOOD.

BOSTON, MASSACHUSETTS,
AUGUST 5, 1882.

SKETCH OF EVENTS INCIDENT TO THE SETTLE-
MENT OF THE PROVINCE OF NEW
NETHERLAND.

The Effect in Holland of the Discoveries along the Shores of America. Special Trading License granted to the Merchants of Amsterdam and Hoorn. The United New Netherland Company. Petition for the Incorporation of the Dutch West India Company. Opposition of the Barneveld Party. The fall of Barneveld, and subsequent Grant of the Company's Charter by the States General. "The Right to Trade with Hudson's Country." Colonization of Fort Orange by the Walloons. Introduction of the Feudal System. "The Charter of Freedoms and Exemptions." The Patroons and their Privileges. The Reformed Protestant Dutch Church of Fort Orange. England seizes New Netherland. The Grant from the Crown to the Duke of York and Albany. The Capitulation signed by Governor Stuyvesant.

THE historical period at which we are to glance, embraces the record of the early settlement of the Knickerbockers, descending from that primitive time when the Province of New Netherland flourished, where now stretch the great commonwealths of New York, New Jersey and Delaware.* It is illustrative of that interesting epoch, which commemorates a civilization that has now passed from among us; of the peaceful days when the Dutch held rule over all that broad and fertile domain, which acknowledged the sway of the States General of Holland.

The eventful tidings brought by Hendrik Hudson of his discoveries along the shores of America, greatly stimulated the maritime enterprise of the merchants of the Netherlands, who speedily sought and obtained legalized authority to trade with that region. This permission was granted by the States General (March 27, 1614), in

---

* Van der Donck, writing in 1649 of New Netherland, says : " It is situate on the North side of America, in the latitude of thirty-eight and one-half degrees, or thereabouts. It is bounded on the North-east by New England ; on the South-west by English Virginia. The Coast extends mostly South-west and North-east, and is sandy alongside the Ocean. The North-west region is still partly unexplored. The South Bay and South River, called by many the second great river of New Netherland, lies in the latitude of 38° 15'. It has two heights or capes, the Northern, called Cape Mey, the Southern, Cape Cornelis, and the Bay itself is called now Port Mey, now Godyn Bay. In the beginning, before any mention was made of the English, after our people had first discovered and explored the most Northerly Part of New Netherland, they erected an Escutcheon on Cape Cod, and took possession. The Boundaries, as we understand, extend from thence to Cape Henlopen."

2

an *Octroy*, giving to the first discoverers " of any new passages, havens, countries or places," by citizens of the United Netherlands, the
exclusive right and privilege of making the first four voyages to such
territory. At this period the United Provinces of Holland, their in-
dependence achieved from the proud dominion of Spain, enjoyed a high
degree of prosperity.* The leading cities, with their great wealth and
commercial prestige, occupied influential rank in Europe, and assured
to the youthful republic a prominent and respected position. The
action of the States General was promptly availed of, therefore, by
a number of the wealthy citizens of Amsterdam and Hoorn, who
proceeded to despatch at once several vessels to the coast of America for purposes of discovery and trade.†

Among the leading navigators who at that time visited our shores,
the most prominent were Adriaen Block, Hendrik Christiaensen and
Cornelis Jacobsen Mey, who explored the region from Cape Cod to
Cape Henlopen, and have left to our day their names impressed upon
various points along that coast.‡ A few months after the passage
of the *Octroy*, the States General formally confirmed its action, by
granting to *The United New Netherland Company*, as provided
by that ordinance, the exclusive right to trade with the settlements
along the coast of America for a period of three years, on or before
January 1, 1615. Immediately thereafter, a building or block house
was erected by Christiaensen for the use of the Company upon an
island in the Hudson, just below the present Albany, to which was

* The Seven United Provinces of Holland, otherwise styled the Northern Netherlands,
dated their separate organization from the celebrated compact formed at Utrecht, in 1579,
when they revolted from the rule of Philip the Second, of Spain, under the lead of William the Silent. From that time until the revolution of 1794, they are to be considered as
one nationality; each province, however, was governed by its own laws, and held substan-
tially the rights of a sovereign state, sending deputies to a general assembly at the Hague,
called the *States General*, which was invested with supreme legislative power, and presided
over by an executive officer who was known as the *Stadtholder*. At this time Holland, or
the Seven United Provinces, was composed of the divisions of *Gelder, Holland, Zealand,
Utrecht, Friesland, Overyssel* and *Groeningen*, together with the territory denominated the
Country of Drent, and *Dutch Brabant*.

† Among the first vessels despatched for trading purposes to the Hudson, which the Dutch
had already begun to call the *Mauritius*, in honor of Prince Maurice, were the galiots *Fortune* and *Tiger*, fitted out in 1612 by three influential and enterprising merchants of Amsterdam, Hans Hongers, Paulus Pelgrom, and Lambrecht van Tweenhuysen, who entrust-
ed their command to Hendrik Christiaensen and Adriaen Block, then just returned from their
joint voyage of discovery thither. Subsequently other merchants of North Holland joined
in the trade. The *Tiger* was accidentally burned while at Manhattan, in the fall of that
year, whereupon Block set about building a small yacht out of the timber furnished by the
forests. The vessel was named the *Onrust* (the Restless), and was launched in the spring
of 1614, from the foot of what afterwards became Beaver Lane. " This pioneer craft," says
De Laet the historian, " was 44½ feet long, 11½ feet wide, and of about 16 tons burden."
See *Appendix, Note A.*

‡ Block Island, at the mouth of Long Island Sound, derives its title from this persevering and indefatigable explorer, while the memory of Mey is perpetuated in the cape which
bears his name.

given the name of Fort Nassau,* and soon after a second trading post was built upon the lower end of Manhattan Island, which was the commencement of the subsequent settlement of New Amsterdam. The sources of trade with the Indian tribes skirting the coast proved abundant, and the returns remunerative to such a degree, that when, in 1618, the trading privilege of the New Netherland Company expired, its exportation of valuable peltries from the country was very extensive, and it became importunate for a renewal of its franchise.† The prospect of obtaining this, however, was for a long time very doubtful, through reason of the reluctance of the States General to longer delegate to a corporation the substantial monopoly of affairs in America, but at length the fierce Arminian controversy, which so violently agitated Holland in 1618–1619, afforded the associated merchants an opportunity to press their scheme with better chances of success.‡

The outcome of this celebrated ecclesiastical contention, resulting, as well known, in 1619, in the utter and complete overthrow of the Arminian element by the Calvinistic party, assisted very materially the petition of the Belgian§ merchants, as it involved the discomfiture and downfall of their most powerful opponent. He was John of Barneveld,‖ the fearless Advocate, the incorruptible

---

* " Fort Nassau," says Brodhead, " a trading house on Castle Island, on the west side of the river, was meant by the Dutch to combine the double purpose of a warehouse and a military defence for the resident traders. It was thirty-six feet long, by twenty-six in width, enclosed by a stockade fifty-eight feet square, the whole surrounded by a moat eighteen feet in width. It was armed with two large guns and eleven swivels or patereroes, and garrisoned by ten or twelve men. It was the first island below Albany, and after 1630, was known as Van Rensselaer's or Patroon's Island."

† Upon January 1, 1618, the Special Trading License granted in 1614 to Gerrit Jacob Witsen and twelve other leading merchants of the cities of Amsterdam and Hoorn, under the title of the United New Netherland Company, for " the exclusive right to trade with Hudson's Country," expired by limitation. It expressly forbade any other party from sailing out of the Provinces to that territory, within the time specified, under pain of confiscation of vessels and cargoes, and a fine of fifty thousand Netherland ducats to the benefit of the grantees of the charter. It was a distinct act of sovereignty over the country between New France (or Canada) and Virginia, which was called New Netherland, a name which it continued to bear for nearly half a century. See Appendix, Note B.

‡ The termination of the Spanish war and the rise of Arminianism, says Motley, were almost contemporaneous. Party lines were sharply drawn by the Stadtholder and his followers, who were opposed to the truce, and many bitter accusations made against those who had favored peace, among which was the charge that they were in sympathy with the religious views formulated by Arminius, which were condemned as rank heresy by the Calvinists. "There are two factions in the land," said Maurice, "that of Orange and that of Spain, and the two chiefs of the Spanish faction are those political and priestly Arminians, Uytenbogaert and Oldenbarneveld."

§ During the protracted struggle against Spanish persecution, and by the inhabitants of the Low Countries, Holland became the asylum of a very large proportion of the prominent and wealthy traders of Belgium. They infused fresh and increased commercial strength into the country of their adoption, and acquired upon its soil great prestige. To these exiled Belgians, of whom perhaps the most prominent was William Usselinex, of Antwerp, belongs the origination of the plan for the foundation of the Dutch West India Company.

‖ John of Barneveld, Advocate of Holland, was the most prominent figure of the States General, and the foremost citizen of the Netherlands, a man who had no superior in statesmanship, in law, in the science of government, in intellectual force and ability. Born at

patriot and statesman, the founder of the Dutch Republic. He adhered firmly to his advocacy of conservative political measures, as well as religious toleration, and at this period, as the head of the party known by his name, was assailed by his enemies with the greatest rancor. His unpopularity with the Belgian faction was greatly increased by his prominent identification with the Dutch East India Company, in whose behalf he strongly opposed granting a charter to a rival organization. These reasons, combined with the ill-concealed hostility of the Stadtholder,* who hated him bitterly, at length resulted in his arrest, protracted imprisonment, and final arraignment before the Synod of Dordtrecht,† which pronounced him guilty (May 13, 1619) of various acts inimical to the State, and sentenced him to the block.

With the death of Barneveld, and the flight to voluntary exile in France of Hugo Grotius, his able and influential compeer, the powerful party which had followed his lead was temporarily disarmed, and its organized opposition to the charter asked for was suspended. Shortly thereafter, the persevering efforts of William Usselinex, united with the good offices of the Stadtholder before the States General, resulted in the grant of its franchise to the Dutch West India Company,‡ with the extraordinary privileges and immunities asked for, and it was formally guaranteed the mercantile control of the American and African shores of the Atlantic.

Amersfoort, in 1547, of the ancient house of Oldenbarneveldt, he had served his country strenuously from youth to old age, with an abiding force of duty, a steadiness of purpose, a broad vision, a firm grasp, and an opulence of resource, such as not one of his compatriots could even pretend to rival. His history was virtually the history of the Dutch Republic, and without his presence and influence, the record of Holland, France, Spain, Britain and Germany might have been essentially modified."—*Motley.*

* Maurice, Prince of Orange, the son of William the Silent. He was an ambitious general, and had acquitted himself with great credit in the fierce struggle with Spain, just closed. He had opposed the conclusion of the treaty of truce with that power, with all the strength he could command, and upon its success arrayed himself at the head of the Orange party, and became Barneveld's greatest enemy, notwithstanding the fact that he had owed his elevation to the office of Stadtholder largely to the efforts of the Advocate.

† The Synod of Dordtrecht convened at the Hague Nov. 13, 1618, and held one hundred and eighty sessions. It pronounced the Arminians "heretics, schismatics, teachers of false doctrine," and declared them " incapable of filling any clerical or academical post." It further proclaimed the Netherland Confession and Heidelburg Catechism to be infallible.—*Motley.*

‡ The charter establishing the Dutch West India Company bears date June 3, 1621. The central power of this vast association was divided among five branches, or chambers, established in the different cities of the Netherlands, the managers of which were styled Lords Directors. Of these, that of Amsterdam was the principal, and to this was intrusted the management of the affairs of New Netherland. The remaining chambers were located respectively in the Meuse, North Holland, Zealand and Friesland. Each of these chambers was a separate society, with members, directors and vessels of its own. The combined capital of the Company was six millions of florins (about two and a half million dollars). Apart from the exclusive trade of Africa, from the tropic of Cancer to the Cape of Good Hope, and of the coast of America, from the Straits of Magellan to the extreme north, the Company was authorized to erect forts and defences, to administer justice and preserve order, declare war and make peace, with the consent of the States General, and with their approbation, to appoint a governor or director-general, and all other officers of the province.
— *O'Callaghan.*

The Amsterdam Chamber,* to which had been assigned the interests of New Netherland, proceeded to erect the territory into provincial dignity, and to initiate efforts towards its development. The Company's charter dated nominally from 1621, but it was not until two years later that it was confirmed in legal corporate privileges. When, in 1623, all obstacles to its sway had been removed, it commenced in earnest the attempt to colonize its new dominion, transporting many emigrants thither  from France, Belgium and the German states, who sought the right of settlement under the liberal provisions of its charter.† The first arrivals were Walloons, or French Protestants from the borders of Belgium, the majority of whom settled on Long Island. A few, however, ascended the Hudson, and in 1623, upon the western bank of that stream, founded a trading settlement, to which, in honor of the Stadtholder, Prince Maurice, they gave the name of Fort Orange. This year may be considered to have been the first of actual colonization in the Province, the traders who had up to that time journeyed thither, having moved from place to place in their traffic with the Indians, and remained only temporarily in the settlement.

Peter Minuit,‡ the first Governor General appointed by the West India Company to represent its authority, arrived at Manhattan in 1626, and at once assumed the duties of his position. Until he came, the powers of government had been vested in a subordinate officer known as *Director*, of whom Adriaen Joris was the first, Cornelis Jacobsen Mey the second, and William Verhulst (Minuit's immediate predecessor) the third. The province prospered greatly

---

* At this period the Directors of the Amsterdam Chamber were Johannes de Laet (the historian), Killiaen Van Rens-elaer, Michael Paauw, Peter Evertsen Hulft, Jonas Witsen, Hendrik Hamel, Samuel Godyn, and Samuel Blommaert. The States General granted it a seal in 1623, with the armorial distinctions of a Count. The seal was a shield bearing a Beaver proper, surmounted by a Count's coronet, with the legend *Sigillum Novi Belgii*.

† Despite the vehement protests of England's minister at the Hague, against " any further settlements or occupations by the Dutch on Hudson's River," the West India Company proceeded to transport colonists thither freely. The first comers were thirty families of Walloons, inhabitants of the frontier between France and Belgium, extending from the Scheld to the river Lys, many of which people, as they professed the reformed faith, had sought asylum in Holland from the persecutions of Spain. Part of these colonists settled on Long Island, at the *Waal-boght*, or Walloons Bay, while the remainder founded Fort Orange. The first white female child born in the province was of Walloon parentage.

‡ Peter Minuit, of Wesel, in the Kingdom of Westphalia, arrived at Manhattan May 4, 1626. " The name of Governor Minuit," says *Valentine*, " is forever identified with the province, through his purchase (May 6, 1626) of the entire island of Manhattan, now New York city, covering an estimated area of twenty-two thousand acres, for a chestful of beads and trinkets given to the Indians, of about the value of sixty guilders, or twenty-four dollars. Henceforth the title became vested in the West India Company." *See Appendix, Note C.*

under his vigorous and energetic control,* and the commercial importance of which it gave abundant promise might have lavishly repaid the Company for the large outlay which had been necessary in its behalf, had not that corporation been subsequently most unfortunate in the policy it elected to pursue, through legislation which proved detrimental and embarrassing to the interests of the valuable territory intrusted to its care.†

In 1629 an act was passed by the West India Company, under the title of " Freedoms and Exemptions granted to all such as shall found Colonies in New Netherland." It provided that any member of the Company who should colonize forty-eight adult persons within the period of four years, in any part of the province, should hold the title of *Patroon*,‡ and enjoy the privilege of selecting any tract

of land, which he might desire, except on Manhattan Island, not, however, to exceed sixteen miles in length. Under this remarkable charter, the first Patroon estate was purchased from the Indians by Samuel Godyn and Samuel Blommaert§ in June of that year, extending along the South (now the Delaware) river. In April, 1630, Killiaen Van Rensselaer,‖ a wealthy merchant of Amsterdam, and

---

* The imports into New Netherland in 1624 amounted to $10,654, and the exports, solely of skins and furs, to about $11,000, while seven years later (in 1631) the imports had risen to $23,000, and the exports to $27,204. "It is computed," says *Valentine*, " that the slothful and loose administration of Van Twiller caused a great unnecessary expense to the Company, the expenses of the province between 1626 and 1644, over and above the returns received therefrom, aggregating over $200,000."

† The introduction of the feudal system into New Netherland, through the famous charter of " *Freedoms and Exemptions*," granted June 7, 1629, was most unfortunate for the future of the Company. The lands selected for each estate " might extend twelve miles in length, if confined to one side of a navigable river, or six miles on each side, and might run as far into the country as the situation of the occupiers will permit." Each patroon was promised " a full title by inheritance, with the right to dispose of his estate by will." In case any patroon " should in time prosper so much as to found one or more cities," he was " to have power and authority to establish officers and magistrates there."—*Holland Doc. II.*

‡ The Patroons of New Netherland were Samuel Godyn and Samuel Blommaert, of *Swanandael*, Killiaen Van Rensselaer, of *Rensselaerswyck*, Michael Paauw, of *Pavonia*, Myndert Myndertsen Van Keren, of *Achter Col* to *Tapaan*, Cornelis Melyn, of *Staaten Island*, Adriaen Van der Donck, of *Colendonck*, Hendrik Van der Capelle, of *One Third of Staaten Island*, Cornelis Van Werckhoven, of *Nevesinck and Tapaan*, City of Amsterdam, of *South River.—New Netherland Register.*

§ The patroon estate of Godyn and Blommaert consisted of a tract of land on " the south corner of the Bay of South River, extending northward about thirty-two miles from Cape Henlopen to the mouth of the said river, and inland about two miles in breadth, being known as *Swanandael.—Brodhead.*

‖ The domain purchased for Killiaen Van Rensselaer, by Sebastian Jansen Krol, consisted of " a tract of land on the west side of the North, or Hudson's River, extending northward from Beeren Island (now Barren Island, 12 miles south of Albany) to Cahoos, and stretching two days' journey into the interior." It embraced in all nearly three quarters of a million acres, and was known as *Rensselaerswyck.* It contained the entire territory comprised

Director in the Company, purchased an extensive tract of country surrounding Fort Orange, which he proceeded to colonize, and gave the name of *Rensselaerswyck*. It is to the efforts of this patroon that is due the settlement of the learned and worthy Dominie Johannes Megapolensis, the first minister of the Reformed Protestant Dutch Church of Fort Orange.* The call asking for the services of this divine in America is signed by the president and scribe

of the Classis of Amsterdam, in Classical Assembly at that city, March 22, 1642. It states that "by the state of navigation in the East and West Indies, a door is opened, through the special providence of God, also in New Netherland, for the preaching of the Gospel of Jesus Christ, for the Salvation of men."

This ancient parish, a cut of whose *third* edifice, formerly standing upon a site now indicated by the junction of the present Broadway and State Street, in Albany, then known respectively as *Handelaer* and *Yonker*, we have printed in the margin, is yet in vigorous existence, occupying the structure known as the North Dutch Church in that city.† We also are fortunately enabled to give a fac-simile of the seal of the early church of Fort Orange, around which cluster so many interesting historical associations. It is still in use, the quaint device inscribed upon it remaining unchanged, while the Society's present corporate title is *The Reformed Protestant Dutch Church, in the City of Albany.*

---

in the present counties of Albany, Columbia and Rensselaer. Killiaen Van Rensselaer, its first patroon, died in 1646. An impression of the official seal of this vast manorial property is given upon page 12. *See Appendix, Note D.*

* This venerable organization, for an imprint of whose unique seal the author is indebted to the courtesy of Joseph W. Russell, Esq., of Albany, one of the trustees of the ancient parish, dates its foundation from a very early period. Its first regular pastor was Dominie Megapolensis, settled in August, 1642, and who served until 1650.

† "The first church was built in 1643, near the fort, in what is now called Church Street," says the Rev. Dr. E. P. Rogers, pastor of its lineal descendant, the North Dutch Church, in 1857. "It was a plain wooden building, thirty-four feet long by nineteen wide, furnished with a pulpit ornamented with a canopy, pews for the magistrates and church officers, and nine benches for the people. Here services were conducted until 1656, when the corner-stone of another and more commodious building was erected upon a site now the junction of State Street and Broadway, the former of which is still preserved in the North Dutch Church in Albany. Some sixty years later, in the pastorate of the Dominie Petrus Van Driessen, a new building was put up, being built around the old church, which was taken down by degrees, as the walls of the later structure were raised. It was built of stone, with a steep pyramidal roof, and a belfry surmounted by a weathercock. Each of its windows contained the coat of arms of some one of the families of the congregation, stained upon the several panes.

A long period of time elapsed, following the recall of the astute Minuit to Holland in 1632, during which Van Twiller, Kieft and Stuyvesant successively held, with varying fortune, administrative sway over the province. But a crisis was at hand in the affairs of New Netherland, which was destined to work an eventful change in the future of the promising colony. In 1658 came the death of Cromwell, succeeded by the downfall of the Commonwealth, and the restoration of the line of Stuart to the English throne signalized the adoption of an aggressive policy towards the Dutch settlements in America.

King Charles the Second, heedless of existing treaties, saw in the flourishing settlement only a coveted opportunity to increase his revenues, by annexation to the dominions of the Crown, and needed not the representations made by several of his loyal subjects, to resolve to possess himself of the fertile plantations along the shores of the Hudson.* He accordingly authorized (March 12, 1664), by royal patent, the grant to his "trusty and well-beloved James, Duke of York and Albany, all that island or islands commonly called by the several name or names of *Matowacks*, or Long Island, situate, lying and being towards the West of Cape Cod and the *narrow Higansetts*, abutting upon the mainland between the two rivers there called or known by the several names of Connecticut and Hudson's River, together also with the said River called Hudson's, and all the land from the West side of Connecticut to the East Side of Delaware Bay,

On the west side were the seats occupied by the governor and the magistrates of the city, while upon the right and left of the pulpit, were the members of the consistory. The seats in the body of the house were occupied by the females, while the prominent burghers and heads of families sat upon the seats around the walls, and the galleries were reserved for the younger male members of the congregation. In front of the desk of the pulpit was placed the hour-glass. It was the custom for the dominie to enter during the singing, and before ascending to the pulpit to stand a moment at the foot of the stairs in silent prayer. The church dissolved its ecclesiastical connection with the religious courts of Holland in the pastorate of Dominie Eilardus Westerlo, in 1772. The religious services were continued in the Dutch language until 1782, when they were first used in English. The old stone church stood till 1805, when its site was sold to the corporation of Albany, and in the spring of 1806 the building was taken down." *See Appendix, Note E.*

* It so happened that three persons had just before this time come over to London, who were admirably qualified to stimulate English animosity against the Dutch colonists in America. These persons were John Scott and George Baxter, who cherished no "good opinion of the law" under which they had smarted in New Netherland, and Samuel Maverick, a zealous Episcopalian, who had formerly lived in tribulation in Massachusetts. All three made zealous professions of loyalty. The result of these witnesses' labors was to satisfy Lord Clarendon, already influenced by the arguments of Sir George Downing, the English envoy at the Hague, that New Netherland belonged to the King, and that it had been "only usurped" by the Dutch, who had "no color of right to pretend to its possession." The Chancellor's opinion, although utterly inconsistent with truth and reason, was conclusive. Yet Charles and his ministry were for some time perplexed whether they should view the Dutch "intruders" as subjects or aliens. At the risk of war it was resolved that the principle announced by Queen Elizabeth and affirmed by Parliament in 1621, should be repudiated and reversed, and New Netherland seized at all hazards.—*Brodhead.*

and also all those several islands called or known by the names of *Martin's Vinyard*, and *Nantukes*, otherwise Nantuckett."*

Preparations were speedily made to substantiate the Duke's claim to the territory thus granted, and in the last days of August, 1664, an English squadron cast anchor off Coney Island,† bearing summons to Stuyvesant‡ to surrender his authority to Richard Nicolls, duly commissioned as the first English governor. The indomitable Director-General proudly spurned the demand, and determined to defend the Company's possessions to the last, but the odds against him were too heavy,§ and finally, realizing the hopelessness of successful resistance, was persuaded by his Council to avoid useless slaughter‖ and avail himself of the liberal terms offered. Upon the morn-

* The inland boundary most consistent with this description was "a line from the head of Connecticut river to the source of Hudson's river, thence to the head of the Mohawk branch of Hudson's river, and thence to the east side of Delaware Bay." The grant was intended to include all the land which the Dutch held there.—*Brodhead.*

† By the orders of the King, an expedition was speedily fitted out against New Netherland, consisting of the *Guinea*, 36 guns, the *Elias*, of 30 guns, the *Martin*, of 16 guns, and the transport *William and Nicholas*, of 10 guns. The fleet, conveying four hundred and fifty troops of the line, set sail from Portsmouth for America on May 25, 1664.—*O'Callaghan.*

‡ Petrus Stuyvesant, a native of Friesland, had formerly been Director of the Company's colony at Curacoa, and received later (July 28, 1646) the appointment of Governor General of the Province of New Netherland, assuming the office May 11, 1647. He was brave and energetic, and the man of all others best calculated to retrieve the fortunes of the colony. But he was also haughty and imperious, and his despotic love of power soon weakened the affection with which he was regarded on his first arrival. With all his faults, however, he was the man for the times, and his firm and vigorous rule contrasts favorably with the ill-judged and capricious conduct of his predecessor. Although loyal to the Company until its dominion ended over the province, he was at heart attached to the interests of the people, with whom he identified himself, after the forced surrender of the city, by taking up his residence among them as a private citizen, dying in August, 1671, and being buried in his family tomb, under a church whose site is now occupied by the parish of St. Mark, in New York city.—*Booth. See Appendix, Notes F and G.*

§ Although there were at this time fifteen hundred souls in New Amsterdam, there were not more than two hundred and fifty men able to bear arms, besides the one hundred and fifty regular soldiers. The city, entirely open along both rivers, was shut on the northern side by a breastwork and palisades, which, though sufficient to keep out the savages, afforded no defence against a military siege. A council of war had reported Fort Amsterdam untenable, for though it mounted twenty-four guns, its single wall of earth, not more than ten feet high and four thick, was almost touched by the private dwellings clustered around, and was commanded, within a pistol shot, by hills on the north, while there were scarcely six hundred pounds of serviceable powder in store. The lesson in St. Luke's Gospel taught Stuyvesant how vain it was, with ten thousand men, to resist him that came with twenty thousand. Yet there was one balm for the director's wounded spirit. Nicolls had voluntarily proposed "to redeliver the fort and city of Amsterdam in New Netherland, in case the difference of the limits of this province be agreed upon betwixt His Majesty of England and the High and Mighty States General." Full power to agree upon articles with the English commandant or his deputies was therefore given by the Dutch director and his council, to Counsellor Johannes de Decker, Commissary Nicholas Varlett and Dominie Samuel Megapolensis, representing the provincial government, and Burgomaster Cornelius Steenwyck, old Burgomaster Oloff Stevensen Van Cortlandt and old Schepen James Cousseau, representing the city.—*Brodhead.*

‖ The twenty-four articles of capitulation declared all the inhabitants of New Netherland to be "free denizens," and secured to them their property. Any persons "might come from Holland and plant in this country," while "Dutch vessels may freely come thither, and any of the Dutch may freely return home, or send any sort of merchandize home, in vessels of their own country. All the Dutch are to enjoy the liberty of their consciences in divine worship and church discipline, as well as their own customs concerning their inheritances," while "the town of Manhattan might choose deputies with free voices in all public affairs." Owners of houses in Fort Orange were "to enjoy their property as all people do where there is no fort." The articles were to be ratified "at eight o'clock upon the morn-

3

ing of Sept. 6, the white flag of parley was displayed from the walls of Fort Amsterdam,* while a few hours later, at the *bouwerie* of Stuyvesant, were settled the articles of capitulation, by virtue of which, New Netherland passed into English hands, and became a part of the territory of the British crown.   Early the following Monday, Sept. 8, the little Dutch garrison, the ensign of Holland flying at its head, marched from the fort with the honors of war.   And as Stuyvesant led his troops down Beaver Street to the place of embarkation, the reign of Charles, of that name the Second, of Great Britain, France and Ireland, King, was proclaimed in his new domain.   Fort Orange and the town of Beverwyck submitted upon the 24th of the same month, and the settlement changed its name to that of *Albany*, the Duke's Scotch title.   The change of rulers was regarded by the inhabitants of the province with comparative indifference, from the fact that the government of the Company had become irksome and annoying, through its arbitrary exactions and monopoly of the most valuable sources of trade.   They were additionally reconciled to the English supremacy by the action of Deputy Governor Nicolls, who declared the estates of the Dutch West India Company confiscated, and had them sold at public vendue.

The control of the settlement was destined, however, temporarily to return to its former proprietors shortly after, when in 1672 England declared war against Holland.   Upon August 6, 1673, nine years after the capitulation, a Dutch fleet entered the harbor, and lying off Staten Island, the redoubtable Evertsen† and Benckes demanded the capitulation of Fort James, formerly Fort Amsterdam, which had been given the name of the new grantee.‡   The English commandant, taken unawares, and being unprovided with adequate means of defence, reluctantly hauled down his flag, and once again the

---

ing of September 8, at the old mill." (This mill, says *Valentine*, was on the shore of the East River, near the foot of what is now known as Roosevelt Street.) "The fort and town called New Amsterdam, upon the isle of Manhattoes, were to be surrendered, the troops to march out with their arms, drums beating, colors flying, and lighted matches."
* The site of Fort Amsterdam was the space enclosed by the streets now called State, Bridge, Whitehall and Bowling Green, in New York city.
† Admiral Evertsen was the eldest son of the famous Admiral Cornelis Evertsen, and one of the most efficient officers who sailed under the colors of the Dutch Republic.
‡ The following is the text of the summons served upon Manning, the English commandant of Fort James, defending the town of New York, in 1673, which we quote from *Valentine*: "Sir: The force of war now lying in your sight, is sent by the High and Mighty States, and His Serene Highness the Prince of Orange, for the purpose of destroying their enemies. We have sent you therefore this letter, together with our trumpeter, to the end that upon sight thereof you surrender to us the Fort called James, promising good quarter; or by your refusal we shall be obliged to proceed both by land and water in such manner as we shall find to be most advantageous for the High and Mighty States. Dated in the Ship *Swanenburg*, anchored between Stanten and Long Island ye 9th Augt (July 30, O. S.), 1673. Cornelis Evertse. Jacob Benckes." *See Appendix, Note II.*

tri-color of the Netherlands waved above their early province. The name of New York gave place for a time to that of *New Orange*, and that of Albany to *Willemstadt*, while Anthony Colve, appointed by the council of war, assumed the duties of governor. It was a fleeting triumph only, and the renewed supremacy of the Dutch was limited to a short period, for with the signature of the Peace of Westminster, in the following year, the settlement was formally restored to English control, and the authority of Holland over the colony it had founded faded away.

So, after a period of fifty years, closed the Dutch dominion in America. An eventful half century had ended, replete with its record of struggle and trial, of victory lost and won. The emblem of the Dutch Republic had been lowered forever over the great dependency which it had suffered to slip from its grasp, and the very name of its former trans-Atlantic province had ceased to exist. New Netherland of the past vanished from the histories of the world, and, transformed, became thenceforth NEW YORK, fairest of all the Anglo-American plantations; and as the splendid possession of an English prince, a new era of prestige and prosperity dawned upon it. Yet, despite the loyal adhesion yielded by the colonists to the new rule so abruptly thrust upon them, their natural attachment for the Fatherland remained warm and true. Steadfast and unswerving in their new allegiance, they ranked among the worthiest subjects of the mightier power which had brought them to its sway, while their posterity through successive generations has looked proudly back to Holland, the land of their kinsmen, and carefully treasured the traditions of the early time.

THE DIRECT ANCESTRY OF THE LATE JACOB WENDELL, OF PORTSMOUTH, N. H.

EVERT JANSEN[1] WENDEL,* the first ancestor of the name who came to these shores, was born in the year 1615,† in the city of Embden,‡ East Friesland (now Hanover), upon the confines of the United Provinces of Holland.§ It was from thence that he emigrated

under the Dutch West India Company to New Netherland, in America, reaching that province in 1640. He was resident at New Amsterdam, on the island of Manhattan (the present site of the city of New

---

* The use of patronymics was common among the Dutch, the father's name being annexed to that of the son or daughter, with the terminations *se* or *sen*, used indiscriminately. Thus, for instance, the name of *Evert Janse Wendel*, Anglicised, means *Evert Wendel*, son of *Jan* (equivalent to *Johannes*, or *John*).

† It is to be understood by the reader that all dates mentioned in this sketch previous to 1751, are *Old Style*.

‡ "The Earldom of *Embdane*," says *Jodocus Hondius*, in an old London work of eminence, of the print of 1635, " is so called from the chieffe Cittie thereof, and now it is called *East Friesland*, because it confineth on *Friesland*. For the *Frieslanders* did not heretofore possess it, but the *Chaueians*, of which *Plinny* and *Ptolemie* make two sorts, the greater and the lesser, so called in regard of their strength. The greater are those that do inhabit the Bishopricke of *Bremes*, the lesser are the *Embdanians* and *Oldenburgians*. The Emperour *Fredericke* the third, Anno 1465, when this province was governed by divers Prafects, did make it a *Comitie* (Earldom), and gave it to one *Vdalrich*. Afterward it had Earles continually, even untill our Time. There are two *Walled Cities* in this *Comitie*, *Embda* and *Arichum*. *Embda*, or *Embdena*, commonly called *Embden*, is the chieffe Cittie of this *Countrie*, and a famous *Mart Towne*, seated by the mouth of the River *Amisia*, having a *Convenient Haven*, the *Channell* whereof is so deepe that great ships may come in under sayle, so that for wealth, for the publicke and private buildings, and for the Multitude of Cittizens, it is known, not onely in Germanie, but also in All Parts of Europe. One of the chieffest Ornaments is the Earle's sumptuous Pallace, the great Church, and the Prætor's house. Heere is wonderfull Plenty of All Things, both for Necessity and Pleasure, which the Haven and the Convenancie of importation of Goods, and also the natural fertility of *Friesland* doth yeeld. The Cittie is so called from the River *Ems*, which *Tacitus* calleth *Amisia*, which divides East from West Friesland."

§ Although Evert Janse[1] Wendel is recorded upon apparently excellent authority as having been of Embden, the author, after the most careful research, announces his conviction that *the family name was not native to that place*. From as thorough a scrutiny as possible of all information in the matter to which he has gained access, he is of the opinion that the first representatives of the family in Embden were originally natives of ancient *Rhynland* or *Delftland* (the present South Holland), who fled thence, as did many other Dutch families of the period, from the religious persecutions of the Duke of Alva, then Regent of Philip II. in the Netherlands. Notwithstanding the fact that the author has yet received no response to the inquiries which he has caused to be instituted in Holland, he believes that the early seat of the name may unquestionably be traced to that portion of the country named above, and he indicates as the most probable localities the cities of *Delft, Haerlem, Leyden* or *Rotterdam*.

TABULAR CHART OF THE ANCESTRY OF THE LATE JACOB WENDELL, OF PORTSMOUTH, N. H.

COMPILED BY JAMES RINDGE STANWOOD.

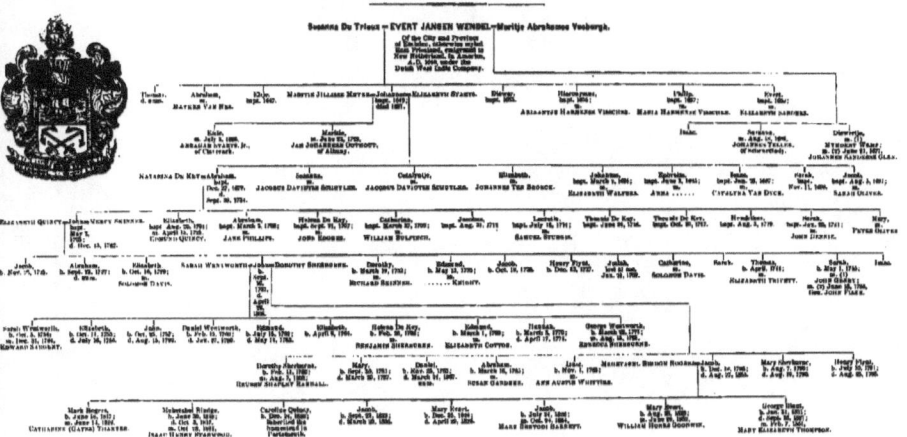

York), for nearly five years subsequent to his arrival,* at the end of that time removing to the growing settlement upon the *Mauritius* (as the Dutch called the Hudson), which had risen around the early trading post of Fort Orange.† The exceptional facilities for traffic with the Indians inhabiting the great tract of forest country extending thence far into the interior, made this place, the commercial centre of the great Patroon estate of *Rensselaerswyck*, a most attractive location for such settlers in the new province as came thither for the purposes of trade, rather than with agricultural intent, although great encouragement was also offered to this interest through the efforts of the patroon.‡ Here Wendel settled, and obtained the requisite license to deal with the Indians§ in beavers and peltries, his first habitation being evidently one of the few houses gathered closely under the guns of Fort Orange.‖ These first dwellings, constituting the earlier portion of the settlement, were removed by order of Governor Petrus Stuyvesant in 1652, when he claimed all land within " two hundred and fifty Rhynland rods "¶ of the fort, as the property of the Dutch West India Company.

Due compensation, however, to the owners of the confiscated property was not omitted, as new patents of land were thereupon granted them upon the site of the later settlement, where now stands the city of Albany. From the records of that city, we ascertain that the grant to Wendel at that time by the worthy governor consisted of " a certain lotte of grounde situate lying and being on y⁰ South side of y⁰ Citty, on y⁰ East side of y⁰ Hill, abutting to y⁰ North of y⁰ Land and Orchard belonging to Isaac Casperse." It is stated by Professor Pearson that his residence was at a later period in a house situated at the corner of James and State (then Yonker) Streets, in Albany, at or about 1700.** He lived in the town during a long period of years, closed by his death in 1709, at an advanced age, and was, we believe, buried under the old church then stand-

---

* In 1642 Evert Janse¹ Wendel lived on Beaver Lane, in New Amsterdam, between the *Breedweg* (Broadway) and *Brugh Straat* (Broad Street).

† The site of the trading-post, or block-house, of Fort Orange, was on the river side between Denniston and Lydius Streets, in the present city of Albany. The settlement of Bever-wyck (or Beaver-town), which at first clustered closely around it, was afterward, in Governor Stuyvesant's time, changed further to the North.—*Brodhead.*

‡ Killiaen Van Rensselaer, the first patroon, judiciously applied his large resources in this direction. He caused a number of farms to be set off on both sides of the river, on which he caused dwelling-houses, barns and stables to be erected, which were stocked with cows, horses, oxen and sheep. Some of these farmers were then valued, and the places assigned them at an annual rent, payable semi-annually in grain, beavers and wampum.—*Munsell's Annals.*

§ Under the rights confirmed to the Patroons by the " Charter of Freedoms and Exemptions," all settlers were bound by oath not to trade with the Indians in furs within the domain of any patroon, unless duly licensed to carry on such trade from that potentate. They were obliged to bring all the furs they purchased to the patroon's magazine, to be sent to Holland by him, he retaining, as his share, one half the profits.

‖ In 1646 the settlement of Beverwyck did not contain over twelve houses.

¶ The Rhynland rod was twelve feet, each foot containing 12.36 English in.

** Evert Janse¹ Wendel lived in a house situate on the west corner of James and State Streets, which was occupied by his son Thomas in 1714.—*Pearson's " First Settlers of Albany."*

ing at the junction of *Yonker and Handelaer Straats* (the present State Street and Broadway) in Albany. It was his fortune to fill various offices of trust and station in the settlement, among which were the positions of *Regerenden Dijaken* of the Reformed Protestant Dutch Church, in 1656, and Magistrate of Fort Orange in 1660–61.

Evert Janse[1] Wendel was married (July 31, 1644) by the Dominie Everhardus Bogardus, in the Reformed Protestant Dutch Church at New Amsterdam,[*] to Susanna, the third daughter of Philip Du Trieux,[†] " *Marshal of New Netherland*," and his wife Susanna, of *Smit's Valley*, in New Amsterdam,[‡] and by her he had issue six children, from whom, together with the offspring of his second subsequent marriage, through matrimonial alliances formed in succeeding generations, may be traced the lineage of the present representatives of the name, and others affiliated therewith, throughout New England and the Middle States. Issue :

    i. THOMAS,[2] bapt ——, eldest son, who inherited his father's house on the Yonker Straat (now State Street) in Albany, and who died there unmarried.

    ii. ABRAHAM,[2] bapt. ——, who m. (April 12, 1698) Mayken Van Nes, of Albany.

    iii. ELSJE,[2][§] bapt. ——, 1647.

2. iv. JOHANNES,[2] bapt. ——, 1649, who m. first, Maritie Jillisse Meyer, of Albany, and second, Elizabeth Staets, of Albany.

    v. DIEWER,[2] bapt. ——, 1653.

    vi. HIERONYMUS,[2] bapt. 1655, who m. Ariaantje Harmense Visscher,[‖] of Albany.

---

  * The first record of a structure fitted for religious uses in New Amsterdam appears in 1625, when a mill for grinding corn, worked by horse power, was erected within the fort, the second story of which was so arranged as to afford accommodations for public worship. The church erected by Governor Kieft in 1642, was of " rock stone, seventy-two feet long, and fifty-two broad, and was built by artisans from Connecticut." At this time most of the houses in New Amsterdam were built of wood, even the chimneys of many of them being made of boards, plastered together at the ends, and the roofs thatched with reeds. The first church-yard, where the ashes of most of the inhabitants of New Amsterdam now lie, was upon the west side of Broadway, upon the rise of ground above Bowling Green, not far north of the present Morris Street.

  † " Philip Du Trieux (or Du Truy)," says Professor Pearson, in his *First Settlers of Schenectady*, " a Walloon, born in 1585, came to New Amsterdam under Minuit's administration, and was granted in 1640 a patent for land in *Smit's Valley*. His wife was Susanna De Scheene, who was living as late as 1654. Issue : *Rebecca*, who married Symon Symmonse Groot; *Sarah*, who married Isaac De Forest; *Susanna*, who married Evert Janse Wendel; *Rachel*, who married first Hendrik Van Bommel, second Dirk Jause De Groot; *Abraham, Isaac*, and lastly *Jacob*, who married Lysbeth Post, of New York. This ancient name has now become transformed into our modern Truex."

  ‡ The boundary of the city was principally defined by the stockades erected in 1653, on the present line of the way then known as *lang de Wall*, now Wall Street. Along the west side of the road, on the shore of the East river, several citizens had established their residence at a very early period. This road, between the city gate and the ferry, at the present site of Peek Slip, was known as *de Smit's Voley*, or the Smith's Valley. The origin of this name is ascribed to the fact that Cornelius Clopper, a blacksmith, established himself on the present corner of Maiden Lane and Pearl Street. The *Smit's Valley* was for a long time the name of that part of the town lying between Wall Street and the present Franklin Square, and was designated by the Dutch as the *Valey* or *Vly*. It was one of the original *straats* established on the first survey of the city, made in 1656.—*Valentine*.

  § It was the custom of the Dutch to carry their children to the church for baptism, and this rite was often performed on the very day of birth, while, except in rare instances, it was generally observed within seven days from that time. The entry, therefore, on the *Doop Boek*, was commonly accepted as the date of birth.

  ‖ The name of Visscher, according to Professor Pearson, was originally *de Vyselaer*, which has been still further corrupted into the modern Fisscher.

      vii. Philip,[2]* bapt. ——, 1657, who m. (June 17, 1688) Maria Harmense
          Visscher. of Albany.
      viii. Evert,[2] bapt. ——, 1660, who m. Elizabeth Sanders, of Albany, and
          died June 16, 1702.

His first wife dying, Evert Janse[1] Wendel was again married (1663) to
Maritje Abrahamse Vosburgh,† of Beverwyck, widow of Tomas Jansen
Mingael, by whom he had further issue, to wit:

      ix. Isaac.[2]
      x. Susanna,[2] bapt. ——, who m. (Aug. 18, 1686) Johannes Teller, of
          Schenectady.
      xi. Diewertje,[2]‡ bapt.——, who m. first, Myndert Wemp,§ of Schenectady,
          and second (June 21, 1671), Johannes Sanderse Glen, of Schenectady.

Upon the death of his second wife, Evert Janse[1] Wendel, according to the
records, married Ariaantje ——, but left no issue by her.

    2. Johannes Wendel[2] (*Evert Janse*[1]), the fourth child of his father by
his first wife (Susanna Du Trieux), was the direct ancestor of that branch
of the family which it is our purpose to trace. Born in New Amsterdam
in 1649, he was
baptized in the Re-
formed Protestant
Dutch Chh. there,
upon February 2
of that year. He
received such edu-
cational advantages as were attainable at that time, and at an early period
became a general trader in Albany. He was successful and prosperous
in his affairs, becoming a wealthy merchant, and achieving a very considerable degree of prominence in the colony. He lived upon the *Yonker
Straat* (or present State Street), in that city, and was called repeatedly
to positions of responsibility and station. He was magistrate in 1684,
captain in the colonial service in 1685, alderman of Albany in 1686, and
in 1690 was empowered, in company with others, with discretionary

---

  * Excellent portraits of descendants of this Philip[2] Wendel, in the next two generations,
are now in possession of Mrs. Harriet Parke, of Albany, a representative of this branch.
  † The daughter of Abraham Pieterse Vosburgh, of the Wynant's Kil, fur trader. He was
the son of Pieter Jacobse Vosburgh, the First Settler of the name who came out from Holland. He received a patent of land in Rensselaerswyck, from Governor Petrus Stuyvesant,
in 1652, south of the stockades of Beverwyck, and west of Fort Orange. The original
grant is now in possession of Mrs. Harriet Parke, of Albany. He married Geertruyd Pieterse Coeymans, and died about 1660, leaving issue of four sons and several daughters.
The ancient township of *Coeymans*, in the County of Albany, indicates the place of residence of the first representatives of the latter family.
  ‡ The baptismal diminutive, *ie* or *je*, was frequently annexed by the Dutch to the name
of a child, as a term of endearment, for instance, as in this case: *Diewertje*, signifying in
English, *little Deborah*.
  § Myndert Wemp, of Schenectady, was appointed Justice of the Peace by Leisler in 1689,
and was killed at the massacre there Feb. 9, 1690.—*Pearson's First Settlers of Schenectady.*

authority to treat with the Five Nations,* and to superintend affairs relating to the defence of Albany.† By the matrimonial alliances which he formed, he added materially to what was already a handsome estate of his own, controlling extensive tracts of country along the Mohawk valley, also in the vicinity of the present Saratoga, and in other parts of the province. He died in 1691, leaving a will‡ which was proved February 9 of that year, of which we have appended a copy to this sketch. He was married first to Maritie Jillisse, the daughter of Gillis Pieterse and his wife Elsie Hendrikse Meyer, of Beverwyck, by whom he had issue two children, to wit :

    i.   ELSIE,[3] bapt. ——, who m. (July 3, 1606) Abraham Staets, jr., of Claverack.§

    ii. MARITIE,[3] bapt. ——, who m. (June 23, 1729) Jan Johannese Oothout, of Albany.

Upon the decease of his first wife, Johannes[2] Wendel married Elizabeth,‖ only daughter of Major Abraham and his wife Katrina (Jochemse) Staes¶ (Staets), of Rensselaerswyck, by whom he had further issue, to wit :

* These distinguished nations, the Mohawks, the Oneidas, the Onondagos, the Cayugas and the Senecas, at the time of the settlement of New York by the Dutch, were firmly bound and concentrated in one, and held the ascendancy over all the North American tribes. Their territory proper extended from Hudson's river on the east to Niagara on the west, from Lake Ontario on the north to the Alleghanies on the south. At one time their actual domain extended from the Sorel south by the great lakes to the Mississippi west, thence east to the Santee, and coastwise back to the Hudson. They were called by the French *Iroquois* (a word according to Charlevoix) derived from *Hiro*, signifying "I have said it," and "*koue*," a term denoting sadness when spoken slowly, and joy when spoken rapidly. The English called them "*The Confederates*, or *Five Nations*, the Dutch *Maquas*, while they themselves knew their title as *Mingoes*." "It is asserted by a writer in 1741," says *Dunlap*, that the confederated Iroquois, or " Five Indian Nations, was established, as the Indians say, one age, or one man's life, before the Dutch settled along the Hudson, and he gives the names of the chiefs who formed the confederacy, to wit: the Mohawk was *Toganawcita*, the Oneida *Otatchertis*, the Onondago *Tatotarpa*, the Cayuga *Togahajon*. The Senecas had two chiefs present, *Gannatarico* and *Satagarureges*. The neutral tribes were either annihilated or incorporated with the Iroquois at or about 1651. The Five Indian Nations were each composed of three tribes, designated individually by the name of some animal, as for example, the Mohawk Nation (which inhabited the valley of the Mohawk) consisted of the *Tortoise*, the *Bear* and the *Wolf*. That part of the Mohawk river which approaches the Hudson marks the situation of the Mohawk tribe. The names of the counties of Oneida and Onondaga give us the location of those two nations, *Onondaga*, or " *the Swamp under the hill*," being the great council ground of the confederated tribes. The Cayugas have impressed their name upon the country of their abode, while the Seneca river points us to territory of that, the farthest of the union, which stretched along the borders of Lake Erie.

† In 1688 Albany was supposed by the French to have had three hundred inhabitants capable of bearing arms. The population in 1698 was three hundred and seventy-nine men, two hundred and twenty-nine women, and eight hundred and three children.

‡ "February 9, 1694. Ye Will of Capt. Joh.[2] Wendel proved by Oaths of Barent Lewis and Gerrit Lansingh, and ye goedvrouw Elizabeth nominated sole executrix."—*Extract from Albany Records.*

§ Claverack, settled by the Dutch at a very early period, received its name, according to Judge Miller, from its situation between four cliffs or hills upon the Hudson, and four others upon its eastern boundary, in the Dutch vernacular, *Klauffer-acht*, or "the place of eight cliffs," while according to another authority the bluffs fronting the river were called the *Klauvers*, or *Clovers*, and as the limits of the town extended thence, it was called *Klauter-rack*, or *Clover-reach.*

‖ After the death of Capt. Johannes[2] Wendel (1691), his widow, Elizabeth (Staes) Wendel, married (April 25, 1695) Capt. Johannes Schuyler, of Albany.—*Pearson's First Settlers of Albany.*

¶ Major Abraham Staes (Staets), surgeon, came to Rensselaerswyck from Holland in 1642, with Dominie Megapolensis, in the galiot *Houttuyn*. He became one of the Council

· 3. iii. ABRAHAM,[3] bapt. Dec. 27, 1678, heir-at-law, who m. (May 15, 1702)
         Katarina, daughter of Theunis and Helena (Van Brugh) De Key,
         of New York.
    iv. SUSANNA,[3] bapt. ——, who m. Jacobus Davidtse Schuyler, of Albany.
    v. CATALYNTJE,[3] bapt.——, who m. Jacobus Davidtse Schuyler, of Albany.
    vi. ELIZABETH,[3] bapt. ——, who m. Johannes Ten Broeck, of Albany.
    vii. JOHANNES,[3*] bapt. Mar. 2, 1684, who m. Elizabeth Walters, of Albany.
    viii. EPHRAIM,[3] bapt. June 3, 1685, who m. Anna ——.
    ix. ISAAC,[3†] bapt. Jan. 28, 1687, who m. Nov. 28, 1717, Catalyna Van Dyck,
         of Albany.
    x. SARAH,[3] bapt. Nov. 11, 1688, and who was living at the time of her
         father's decease in 1691.
    xi. JACOB,[3‡] bapt. Aug. 5, 1691, who removed to Boston, Mass., and who
         m. (Aug. 12, 1714) Sarah Oliver, of Cambridge.

3. ABRAHAM[3] WENDELL§ (*Johannes,*[2] *Evert Janse*[1]), eldest son and heir-
at-law of his father Johannes[2] by his second wife (Elizabeth Staets), was
born in Albany in 1678,
and when of age removed
to New York, where he
became an importer of considerable degree, engaged
in trade with the leading

in 1643, and President of the board in 1644, at a salary of 100 florins (about $40). He ob-
tained license to trade in furs, and had also a considerable bouwerie (farm), at the same
time pursuing the practice of his profession. He was the ancestor of the *Staats* of the present day. He married Katrina Jochemse, by whom he had issue five children, to wit:
Jacob, who m. Ryckie ——; *Abraham,* b. 1665, who m. Elsie Wendel; *Samuel,* who m.
first, ——, second (May 7, 1709), Catharina Hawarden; *Jochem,* who m. Antje Barentse,
and *Elizabeth,* who m. Johannes[2] Wendel.—*Ibid.*
    * This Johannes[3] Wendell, to whom, by the will of his father Johannes,[2] descended
Steen Rabie (or Stone Arabia) the present site of Lansingburgh, N. Y., had a son Johannes
(born February 8, 1708) who removed to Boston, Mass., where he married (Nov. 11, 1731)
Mary, first child of James and Rebecca (Lloyd) Oliver. He died at Boston, February,
1772, leaving a will, of which his widow was appointed sole executrix.
    † Hendrik Van Dyck, first of the name in this country, came to New Amsterdam from
Holland in 1645. He lived, according to *Valentine,* in 1680, upon the *Heere Straat* (the
present Broadway). He was in the service of the Dutch West India Company, and at a
later period officiated as attorney-general under Stuyvesant. He died in 1688, leaving a
wife (Diewertje Cornelise Van Dyck) and issue.
    ‡ Jacob[3] Wendell (bapt. Aug. 5, 1691), the youngest son of Johannes[2] and Elizabeth
(Staes) Wendel, was the first of the name to remove to New England, and came to Boston
when a youth, receiving his business education in the counting-house of Mr. John Mico, a
well known Boston merchant of the period. At the close of this connection he entered
into business upon his own account, accumulated a handsome estate, and became one of the
most prominent citizens of his day. He was uncle to John[4] Wendell, the son of his eldest
brother Abraham, who came to Boston at a later period, and became associated with him
in business. He was of his Majesty's Council from 1737 to 1760, commander of the Ancient and Honorable Artillery 1735 and 1745, and in 1733 director of the first banking
institution in the province. In evidence of the fact that he was not forgetful of the early
Dutch settlement, where dwelt so many of his kindred, may be mentioned the possession,
by the old church in Albany, of an antique christening basin of coin silver, bearing the
following inscription : *De Gift van Jacob Wendell tot Boston, voor de Duytse Kerck tot Albany, Anno* 1719. The Hon. Col. Wendell lived at the corner of School and Common (the
present Tremont) Sts., and married (Aug. 12, 1714) Sarah, daughter of Dr. James and Mercy
(Bradstreet) Oliver, of Cambridge, by whom he had issue twelve children, four sons and
eight daughters. His son Oliver (born March 5, 1733) married (1762) Mary, daughter of
Edward and Dorothy (Quincy) Jackson. Sarah Wendell, his daughter, married the Rev.
Dr. Abiel Holmes, of Cambridge, and their fourth child (born Aug. 29, 1809) is Dr. Oliver
Wendell Holmes. Margaret, the twelfth child of Hon. Jacob[3] Wendell, married (June 12,
1760) William Phillips, of Boston, and their third child, John Phillips (born Nov. 26, 1770),
married Sarah, daughter of Thomas and Sarah (Hurd) Walley, whose eighth child (born
Nov. 29, 1811) is our present fellow citizen, Wendell Phillips, in whose possession is an
admirable portrait, by Smibert, of the Hon. Jacob[3] Wendell, his ancestor.
    § In this generation the family changed the orthography of their name to *Wendell.*
    4

cities of Holland, and also with those of New England. Inheriting a large share of the handsome estate of his father, he increased his possessions very materially by marriage, and was an extensive land owner in the province. He was a merchant of liberality and generous character, and a worthy citizen. Retiring from business later in life, he removed to Boston, Mass., with his family, dying there (September 28, 1734), and was buried in the family tomb of his son, John[4] Wendell, numbered 55 in the Granary Burial Ground on Tremont Street in that city. He married* (May 15, 1702) Katarina, eldest daughter of Theunis and his wife Helena (Van Brugh)† De Key,‡ of New York, by whom he had issue of twelve children, to wit:

4. i.   John,[4] bapt. May 2, 1703, who m. (Nov. 10, 1724) Elizabeth, daughter of Hon. Edmund and his wife Dorothy (Flynt) Quincy, of Braintree, Mass.

ii.   Elizabeth,[4] bapt. Aug. 20, 1704, who m. (April 15, 1725) Edmund Quincy, of Boston, and died there Nov. 7, 1769.

iii.   Abraham,[4] bapt. March 3, 1706, who m. Jane Phillips, and died April 17, 1741.

iv.   Helena De Key,[4] bapt. Sept. 21, 1707, who m. John Rogers, and died at Jamaica, West Indies.

---

* This branch of the Wendells may trace descent on the maternal side from *Anneke Janse*, through this marriage of Abraham[3] Wendell with the great-granddaughter of that celebrated character.

† The Hon. Johannes Pieterse Van Brugh, born in the city of Haerlem in Holland, in 1624, and prominently connected with the Dutch West India Company, lived in New Amsterdam, of which he was Burgomaster in 1656, and again in 1673, when the Dutch retook the city from the English, and named it *New Orange.* He was a wealthy merchant, and a member of the *Groot-Burgerrecht,* or *Great Citizenship,* of New Amsterdam in 1657, which then numbered only twenty. According to historians of the period he resided upon *The water zyde,* the location of his house being upon the west side of the present Pearl Street in New York, between Wall and William Streets. He married (March 29, 1658) *Katrina Roeloffse,* daughter of the celebrated Anneke (or Annetje) Janse, by whom he had issue as follows: *Helena* (bapt. April 4, 1659); *Helena* (bapt. July 28, 1660), who married (May 26, 1680) Theunis De Key; *Anna* (bapt. Sept. 10, 1662), who married (July 2, 1684) Andries Grevenract; *Catharina* (bapt. April 19, 1665), who married (March 19, 1688) Hendrik Van Rensselaer; *Petrus* (bapt. July 15, 1666), who married (Nov. 2, 1688) Sara Cuyler; *Johannes* (bapt. Nov. 22, 1671), who married (July 9, 1696) Margarita Provoost; and lastly, *Maria* (bapt. Sept. 20, 1673), who married Stephen Richards.

‡ The family of *De Key* was represented at an early period among the settlers of New Amsterdam. The first mention of the name in connection with the colony is found in the archives of the Dutch West India Company at the Hague, from which it appears that Jacob De Key, of Haerlem, Holland, was one of the Lords Directors of the Amsterdam Chamber, previous to 1634. Willem De Key was Receiver General of New Amsterdam in 1644, and was, we believe, the first of the name upon Manhattan. Jacob Theunisen De Key is found in New Amsterdam prior to 1660. He was, probably, a brother of Willem, and lived in 1664 upon *Beurs Straat,* in that city, occupying a house upon the present east side of what is now Whitehall Street, between Pearl and Beaver. " He was esteemed," says *Valentine,* " as a citizen of probity and honor, and was prominent in the councils of the church. He died in the possession of a large property, leaving, among other issue, two sons, Theunis and Jacobus, from whom descend the representatives of the name." Theunis lived upon the *Heeren Graeht* (the present Broad Street), and married (May 26, 1680) *Helena Van Brugh,* by whom he had issue twelve children, to wit: *Katarina* (bapt. March 15, 1681), who married Abraham Wendell ; *Helegonda* (bapt. Nov. 1, 1682), who married Jacobus Bayard; *Jacobus* (bapt. Aug. 31, 1684), who died Nov. 29, 1719; *Lueretia* (bapt. Aug. 8, 1686), who died June 11, 1711; *Johannes* (bapt. March 4, 1688), died July 10, 1689; *Johannes* (bapt. Nov. 13, 1689), died 1756; *Helena* (bapt. Dec. 6, 1691), died same year; *Rachel* (bapt. April 9, 1693), died 1694; *Hendrikus* (bapt. Sept. 22, 1695), died 1719; *Petrus* (bapt. 1697), died 1717; *Helena* (bapt. April 22, 1699), died 1700; and lastly *Helena* (bapt. Feb. 1, 1702), who married (Sept. 1, 1727) Samuel Sheffield, and at his death again married (Aug. 11, 1744) G[d]. Haeghoort. A quaint silver-mounted cane, with the inscription, *Teunis De Key,* 1697, is in the possession of Miss Caroline Quincy Wendell, of Portsmouth, N. H.

v.   CATHARINA,[4] bapt. March 27, 1709, who m. William Bulfinch, of Boston.
vi.   JACOBUS,[4] bapt. Aug. 31, 1712.
vii.   LUCRETIA,[4] bapt. July 18, 1714, who m. Samuel Sturgis, of Barnstable, Mass., and died there March, 1752.
viii.   THEUNIS DE KEY,[4] bapt. June 21, 1716, who died young.
ix.   THEUNIS DE KEY,[4] bapt. Oct. 30, 1717.
x.   HENDRIKUS,[4] bapt. Aug. 3, 1719.
xi.   SARAH,[4] bapt. Jan. 20, 1721, who m. John Dennie, of Boston, Mass.
xii.   MARY,[4] who m. Peter Oliver.

4. JOHN[4] WENDELL (*Abraham,*[3] *Johannes,*[2] *Evert Janse*[1]), eldest son of Abraham[3] and his wife Katarina (De Key) Wendell, was born in New York in 1703, and baptized in the Reformed Protestant Dutch Church there, May 2 of that year. He was educated in that province, remaining there for some years, but subsequently removed to Boston, Mass., where he entered upon business. He was a merchant and importer, doing an extensive traffic with foreign parts, being associated in copartnership with his, uncle, the Hon. Jacob[3] Wendell, the firm having a large wholesale warehouse located in 1754 upon Merchants Row,* then the commercial centre of the West India trade, situated at that time upon the edge of tide-water. The firm of Jacob[3] Wendell & Co. was, however, a great sufferer by the destructive fire which visited Boston on March 20, 1760, sustaining, in common with numerous others, heavy losses from which it never fully recovered. John[4] Wendell was a citizen of high standing and respectability, and the contemporary in mercantile circles of William Phillips, Benjamin Greene, Josiah Quincy, John Erving, Thomas Hancock and others, and while he does not appear to have been called to public station, took, notwithstanding, great interest in the advancement of colonial affairs. He was repeatedly commissioned in the military establishment of the province, and ranked as a field officer at the time of his death. He was identified with the Ancient and Honorable Artillery Company from 1733, was Ensign of that corps in 1735, and its commander in 1740. His mansion stood in 1760, upon the corner of Queen (the present Court) and Trea-mount† (now Tremont) Streets, facing in that day upon the latter.

---

* The commercial street upon which the warehouse of the firm of Jacob[3] Wendell & Co. was located in 1754, dates the formal adoption of its name to a meeting of the selectmen of the town of Boston, held May 3, 1708, at which the following vote was passed : *Ordered*, that the Streets, Lanes and Alleys of this Town, as they are now bounded and named, be recorded in the Town Book." In a transcript of this record we find it declared that " the Way leading from Madam Butler's corner, at y⁰ Lower End of King (the present State) street, to the Swinging Bridg, and from thence to y⁰ Lower End of Woodmansie's Wharfe, shall be called *Merchants Row*." The bridge referred to crossed the cove running inland at that day above the present Faneuil Hall, known as the Town Dock, in the vicinity of the present Faneuil Hall Square.

† The street denominated in the early records *Trea-mount* or *Tra-mount*, which forms the lower end of the Tremont Street of our day, was defined in 1708 as " The Way leading from y⁰ mansion house of y⁰ Late Simon Lynde Esq⁰., by Capt. Southbacks, extending as

The building now standing upon that site, at present occupied by lawyers'
offices, and the store of Messrs. S. S. Pierce & Co., is the identical structure, although it has since undergone very material alterations.* A tablet
inserted in the Court Street end commemorates the fact of its occupa-
tion by Washington upon the occasion of his visit to Boston in 1789.
John[4] Wendell married (November 10, 1724) Elizabeth, second daughter
of Hon. Edmund and his wife Dorothy (Flynt) Quiney,† of Braintree, by
whom he had issue of fifteen children, to wit :

  i. JACOB,[5] b. Nov. 23, 1725.
  ii. ABRAHAM,[5] b. Sept. 23, 1727, who died unmarried at Boston, April 13,
    1752.
  iii. ELIZABETH,[5] b. Oct. 16, 1729, who m. Solomon Davis, of Boston.
 5. iv. JOHN,[5] b. Sept. 10, 1731, who m. (June 20, 1753) Sarah Wentworth,
    of Portsmouth, N. H., and at her death again m. (Aug. 20, 1778)
    Dorothy Sherburne, of Portsmouth, N. H.
  v. DOROTHY,[5] b. March 19, 1733, who m. Richard Skinner, of Marblehead,
    Mass.
  vi. EDMUND,[5] b. May 13, 1735, who m. —— Knight, at Antigua, West
    Indies, and died there (March 2, 1793), leaving no issue.
  vii. JACOB,[5] 2d, b. Oct. 19, 1736, who died in Boston.
  viii. HENRY FLYNT,[5] b. Dec. 23, 1737, who died on the voyage from Jamaica,
    West Indies.
  ix. JOSIAH,[5] b. ——, who was lost at sea on the voyage from Monte Cristo,
    Jan. 21, 1762.
  x. CATHARINE,[5]‡ b.——, who m. Solomon Davis, of Boston, and died there
    April 7, 1805.
  xi. SARAH,[5] b. ——.
  xii. THOMAS,[5] b. April —, 1744, who m. Elizabeth Trivett, of Marblehead,
    Mass.
  xiii. SARAH,[5] b. May 1, 1745, who m. John Gerry, of Marblehead, Mass.,
    and at his death again m. June 18, 1786, Gen. John Fiske, of Sa-
    lem, Mass.
  xiv. ISAAC,[5] b. ——.
  xv. A child,[5] unnamed, stillborn.

---

far as Collo. Townsends corner." It will thus be seen that it extended only as far south
as School Street, its continuation being the way past the burial-ground (the Granary),
which was then known as Common Street.

 * Among the letters of the late Jacob Wendell, of Portsmouth, N. H., I find the following reference to John Wendell's residence in Boston. He says : "My grand-father's house
in Boston was at the head of Prison Lane, next to old Dea. Henchman's, at the corner going
to the Common, by Captain Emery's estate on Tremont Street. Deacon Henchman's house
was later occupied by Rev. S. K. Lothrop. The prison, as well remembered by many of
the present generation, stood upon the present site of the Court House, and the part of
Court Street extending by the front of the prison, from Washington Street to Tremont, was
called Prison Lane."

 † The Hon. Edmund Quincy, a citizen of great prominence and influence in the province,
who married (1701) Dorothy, daughter of Rev. Josiah and Esther (Willet) Flynt, of Braintree. He was the grandson of Edmund Quincy (born in England, 1602), who arrived in
Boston, Mass., Sept. 4, 1633. He graduated at Harvard College in 1699, and subsequently
was in the public service nearly all his life. He was of His Majesty's Council, Colonel of
the Suffolk Regiment of yeomanry, a magistrate of the province, and one of the Justices of
the Supreme Court. In 1737 he was appointed Agent for the province at the Court of Great
Britain, to settle the boundary line between Massachusetts and New Hampshire, but died
in London, England, February 23, 1738. His death was deeply lamented by his country-
men, and the General Court of Massachusetts, as an acknowledgment of his public services,
granted to his heirs a thousand acres of land in the town of Lenox, and ordered a monument
to be erected over his grave in Bunhill-fields, London, at the expense of the province, with
an inscription terminating thus : "He departed the delight of his own people, but of
none more than the Senate, who as a testimony of their love and gratitude, have directed
this epitaph to be inscribed on his monument."

 ‡ Solomon Davis married two sisters successively.

John⁴ Wendell, upon the death of his first wife Elizabeth, was again married (1751) to Mercy Skinner, of Marblehead, but we find no record of his having had issue by her. He died Dec. 15, 1762.

5. JOHN⁵ WENDELL (*John,⁴ Abraham,³ Johannes,² Evert Janse¹*), fourth son of John⁴ and his wife Elizabeth (Quincy) Wendell, was born in Boston September 10, 1731. He received the requisite preparation for Harvard College, entered that institution at the age of fifteen, and was graduated thence in 1750. Shortly afterwards he removed to Portsmouth, in the Province of New Hampshire, where he established himself as a real estate lawyer and conveyancer, and became subsequently possessed of large landed interests. He held professional and social relations with many of the leading citizens of the time, who were prominent during the Revolutionary period, among whom we note the names of Hancock, Quincy, Otis, Langdon, Livingston, Morris, Hamilton, Jay, and Ethan Allen, while he was the warm personal friend of Hon. Elbridge Gerry, Gen. Philip Schuyler, Gen. Peter Gansevoort, Gen. John Sullivan and Thomas Dudley. He was a man of vigorous mind and energetic disposition, and it may be justly said of him that he contributed freely from his moderate fortune, as well as by his pen, towards sustaining the stand early taken in the province against the arbitrary exactions of the Crown. Although repeatedly solicited to occupy official station, he persistently declined so doing, preferring to remain apart from public life, and unbiassed in his political opinions. He was a ready speaker and writer, and a man of considerable scholastic taste, in recognition of which he received the degree of Master of Arts from Yale College in 1768, and from Dartmouth in 1773. He died in Portsmouth, April 29, 1808, in his seventy-seventh year. John⁵ Wendell married (June 20, 1753) Sarah, eldest daughter of Daniel* and Elizabeth (Frost) Wentworth, of Portsmouth, by whom he had issue of eleven children, to wit:

 i. SARAH WENTWORTH,⁶ b. Oct. 5, 1751, who m. (Dec. 31, 1781) Edward Sargent, of Portsmouth.
 ii. ELIZABETH,⁶ b. Oct. 11, 1755; died July 16. 1756.
 iii. JOHN,⁶ b. Oct. 25, 1757; died Aug. 15, 1799, unmarried.
 iv. DANIEL WENTWORTH,⁶ b. Feb. 15, 1760; died Jan. 27, 1780.
 v. EDMUND,⁶ b. July 15, 1762; died May 14, 1763.
 vi. ELIZABETH,⁶ b. April 9, 1764.
 vii. HELENA DE KEY,⁶ b. Feb. 28, 1766, who m. Benjamin Sherburne, of Portsmouth.
 viii. EDMUND,⁶ b. March 4, 1769, who m. Elizabeth Cotton.

---

* Daniel Wentworth (born Jan. 5, 1715), a merchant of Portsmouth, N. H., who died there June 19, 1747. He was a descendant through Lieut. Governor John of Portsmouth (born Jan. 16, 1671), and Samuel of Dover (born 1641), of Elder William Wentworth (born 1616), of Alford, co. Lincoln, the first English emigrant of the name to America, who settled at Exeter, N. H., in 1639.— *Wentworth Genealogy.*

  ix. HANNAH,[6] b. March 3, 1770; died April 17, 1771.
   x. GEORGE WENTWORTH,[6] b. March 22, 1771, who m. (Aug. 15, 1795)
     Rebecca Sherburne.
  xi. A child,[6] unnamed, stillborn.

  Upon the decease of his first wife (Nov. 17, 1772) John[5] Wendell again married (Aug. 20, 1778) Dorothy, second daughter of Judge Henry and his wife Sarah (Warner) Sherburne,* of Portsmouth (b. Aug. 20, 1752), by whom he had further issue, to wit:

  xii. DOROTHY SHERBURNE,[6] b. Feb. 11, 1780, and who m. (Aug. 7, 1802)
     Reuben Shapley Randall.
  xiii. MARY,[6] b. Sept. 30, 1781, and died March 20, 1787.
  xiv. DANIEL,[6] b. Nov. 25, 1783, and died unmarried March 24, 1807.
  xv. ABRAHAM,[6] b. March 18, 1785, who m. Susan Gardner, of Portsmouth,
     and died there March 27, 1865.
  xvi. ISAAC,[6] b. Nov. 1, 1786, who m. (1809) Ann Austin Whittier, of Dover,
     N. H.; removed (1830) to Bustleton, Pa., and died there.
6 . xvii. JACOB,[6] b. Dec. 10, 1788, who m. (Aug. 15, 1815) Mehetabel Rindge
     Rogers, of Portsmouth, and died there on Aug. 27, 1865.
  xviii. MARY SHERBURNE,[6] b. Aug. 7, 1790, who died Aug. 19, 1790.
  xix. HENRY FLYNT,[6] b. July 10, 1791, who died Aug. 25, 1796.

  6. JACOB WENDELL[6] (*John*,[5] *John*,[4] *Abraham*,[3] *Johannes*,[2] *Evert Janse*[1]), the sixth child of John by his second wife, Dorothy (Sherburne) Wendell, was born in Portsmouth, N. H., December 10, 1788. Educated in his native town, he entered business life on leaving school, and acquired, within a comparatively short period, such thorough mercantile training and familiarity with commercial matters, as enabled him a few years later, to become a merchant and importer on his own account, in the Russian and West India trade. In this pursuit he was remunerated by abundant returns, and, with judicious and conservative management, he rapidly accumulated what was for those days a handsome property, becoming a prominent and respected citizen.

  The responsibilities of affairs unquestionably tend, in a greater or less degree, towards absorption of the social and domestic tastes. Too often is the man of business, engrossed in watchful scrutiny of his interests, and

  * The Hon. Henry Sherburne (born April 4, 1709), a citizen of abundant wealth, prominent station and influence in the Province of New Hampshire, who married (Oct. 2, 1740) Miss Sarah, daughter of Daniel and Sarah (Hill) Warner, of Portsmouth. He graduated at Harvard College in 1728, was Clerk of the Courts of the Province from 1729 to 1739, and from 1745 for twenty-one years representative from Portsmouth to the Provincial Assembly, of which he was Speaker the last ten years. He was delegate to the Colonial Congress at Albany in 1754, in 1765 was made Chief Justice of the Superior Court, and in 1766 was appointed Counsellor. He was great-grandson through *Henry* (born 1674), *Samuel* (born 1638), of the first American ancestor, *Henry Sherburne* (born 1611), who emigrated from Hampshire, England, to the Piscataqua in 1632, who was the second son of *Joseph Sherburne*, of Odiham, Hampshire (died 1621), who was the lineal descendant in a younger branch, through *Henry* (born 1555), of Oxford; *Hugh* (born 1534), of Haighton; *Richard* (born 1510), of Bayley and Haighton; *Richard* (born 1483), of Wiswall, the second son of *Sir Richard Sherburne*, Knight, of Stonyhurst, in the town of Aighton, Lancashire (born 1465), the ninth in regular descent, to whom had fallen that princely inheritance.—*MS. of Edward Raymond Sherburne.*

wrapped in contemplation of fresh plans for added influence and profit, inclined to subordinate to an indifferent place those cheering and brightening associations of home and its surroundings, which do so much to render life desirable and happy. This could not be said of Mr. Wendell. He possessed strong points of character. He was energetic, clear-headed and prudent, of sterling integrity and honor; devoted to his business, and unceasingly faithful to its demands upon him; but he did not allow it to mar or lessen the force of social ties. He was a loving and affectionate husband and father, a generous brother and an indulgent friend, and it was in the congenial domestic circle that he sought and found his respite from the care and bustle of business life.

It was in 1815 that he embarked with his brother Isaac[6] Wendell and others in the enterprise of establishing and operating some of the earlier mills founded in New Hampshire for the manufacture of cotton cloth.* The industry of weaving textile fabrics was then in its infancy upon this side the Atlantic, very little being known here at that period of the improved machinery patented in Great Britain, which was prohibited by the government from exportation abroad. The embryo manufacturers purchased, through Daniel Webster, then resident in Portsmouth, several fine water privileges, the first acquisition being the estate in Dover, known as the Waldron farm, upon which they erected successively several structures. In the fall of 1821, the first mill was ready to commence operations, and its machinery was started in control of a skillful superintendent, under such favorable auspices, and with such satisfactory results, that two years later another mill was built upon the Salmon Falls river, upon a site purchased of Mr. Gershom Horn, which was the pioneer factory of the Great Falls corporation.

For some time everything went prosperously. The mills earned a handsome profit upon the capital invested, the stock advanced to a premium, and all seemed to augur well for the future, when the notable commercial

---

* This undertaking was first initiated by some gentlemen of Dover, at what was known as the *Upper Factory*, where they were at that time spinning yarn and also making nails. Isaac Wendell, my father, entered warmly into the enterprise, and enlisted in its interests, and in those of the new mills established at Dover, and subsequently at Great Falls, his brother Jacob Wendell and others, with his partner, John Williams, of Dover. The location and rise of the Great Falls Manufacturing Company dates from 1823, the legislative act granting it incorporation bearing date June 11 of that year. The inspection of mechanical details in the factory at Dover was intrusted to William Blackburn, an experienced weaver from the city of Manchester, in England, while Isaac Wendell occupied the position of agent, and exercised a general supervision over the interests of the mills. Of the working capacity of these factories some idea may be gained when we state that the first year (1821) three thousand spindles were put in operation in the wooden mill at Dover, since removed, while the total number operated at both places exceeded thirty thousand. The bricks necessary for these buildings were made on the ground, while much of the iron work needed was furnished by a small furnace erected on the Bellamy river. The mills made shirtings, print cloths and sheetings, and the annual production was very large. Twelve to fifteen hundred operatives were employed on the corporation, while the amount of money disbursed monthly, exclusive of the cost of cotton, amounted to a large sum. In 1825 the Company attempted the manufacture of woolen cloth and carpets, erecting a mill for that purpose, but it soon relinquished this project, and put the new factory also upon cotton.— *MS. of Ann Elizabeth Wendell.*

panic of 1827–28 swept the country, and one mercantile crash succeeded another. The destruction of all confidence in business credit and financial strength was rapid and wide-spread, involving on all sides extended commercial ruin, among which was the failure of the Great Falls Manufacturing Company, and the consequent precipitation of heavy losses upon Jacob⁶ Wendell, with others, which were terribly severe. The shock of this calamity, though it very seriously and almost hopelessly crippled him financially, did not, however, cause him utter discouragement. While overwhelmed by the sudden and terrible revulsion of fortune, his spirit was not crushed, and accepting the unwelcome circumstances in which he was placed, he devoted his energies, for the long years which were to come, towards the amelioration of the catastrophe.

He held firm and pronounced religious convictions, being from early years connected with the well known South Parish Society* of Portsmouth. He united with its church membership during the memorable pastorate of the Rev. Dr. Nathan Parker,† between whom and himself existed the most cordial friendship, while the active interest he evinced in all relating to the welfare and prosperity of the ancient parish in which he was brought up, continued to the time of his decease. He had marked taste for historical and antiquarian matters, and was a corresponding member of the New England Historic, Genealogical Society from 1847. He was married (Aug. 15, 1816) to Mehetabel Rindge,‡ only daughter of Mark and Susanna Ro-

---

* The records of the religious organization known as *The South Parish*, of Portsmouth, N. H., run back into the early annals of the province, being contemporary with that period when Churchman and Puritan strove zealously for ecclesiastical control of the settlements along the Piscataqua. "Its first pastor, the Rev. John Emerson," says Rev. Dr. A. P. Peabody, in a discourse descriptive of its history, in 1859, "was installed in March, 1715. Its first house of worship was the building which had been erected in 1658, upon the hill below the South Mill Bridge, at the present junction of Water and South Streets. This was a substantial structure, sixty feet by thirty, with galleries, a low belfry and a bell, the windows with diamond panes, set in lead. It originally had no pews; the men and women being seated on opposite sides of the main floor, according to their respective claims to precedence, and the boys and girls occupying places in opposite galleries. Pews were subsequently built in various parts of the house by individual worshippers. In 1731, the edifice known as the Old South Meeting-house was built, on a site bequeathed to the parish by the John Pickering who had been so largely instrumental in its separate organization." Here, successive to the pastorate of Rev. Mr. Emerson, who died in office in 1732, were conducted the ministries of Rev. William Shurtleff, Rev. Job Strong, and Rev. Dr. Samuel Haven. In the pastorate of the next incumbent, Rev. Dr. Nathan Parker, came that religious change which stirred New England so profoundly, which may be defined as "the Channing movement," initiated at Baltimore in 1819, and to which the parish, in common with many others, thenceforth transferred its allegiance. *The Old South* was vacated in 1826, when the society completed and occupied the present Stone Church, but it stood until 1863, being used during a portion of the time for religious purposes, and was then taken down.

† The Rev. Nathan Parker, D.D., fifth minister of the South Parish. Born at Reading, Mass., in 1782, he graduated at Harvard College in 1803, and Sept. 14, 1808, was ordained at Portsmouth, succeeding the Rev. Dr. Samuel Haven. He was a man of great ability and talent, the peer of any clergyman of his time, and was greatly loved and esteemed by all who knew him. After a most successful pastorate of twenty-five years, during which the prosperity of the parish was most materially increased, he died in office Nov. 8, 1833.

‡ The family of *Rindge* is of English origin, the first representative of the name of whom we have record in Massachusetts being found in the person of *Daniel Rindge*, first of Roxbury (1639), who removed to Ipswich in 1648. He married Mary Kinsman, and died in February, 1661, leaving among other issue, three sons, *Daniel, Roger* and *Isaac*, of whom the present bearers of the name are the descendants. Isaac married Elizabeth Dutch, and their eldest son *John Rindge* (born June 1, 1695), of Portsmouth, N. H. (1710), married Ann,

gers.* of Portsmouth, with whom he lived most happily for a long period of years, only terminated by her death, which occurred April 30, 1859.   They were blest with a family of eight children, six of whom they lived to see grow to years of maturity, and occupy reputable and useful relations in society. Jacob[6] Wendell survived his wife six years, dying at the homestead on Pleasant Street, Portsmouth, Aug. 27, 1865.   Issue :

i.   MARK ROGERS,[7] b. June 18, 1817, who removed to Boston, who m. (June 13, 1849) Catharine (Gates) Thaxter, of that city, and now resident there.

ii.   MEHETABEL RINDGE,[7] b. June 30, 1818, who m. (Oct. 28, 1844) Isaac Henry Stanwood, of Woodville, Mississippi, and died in Cincinnati, Ohio (Oct. 3, 1847), and was buried at Portsmouth, N. H., leaving issue one child, James Rindge.

iii.   CAROLINE QUINCY,[7] b. Dec. 24, 1820, unmarried, who inherited the homestead in Portsmouth, and resident there in 1882.

iv.   JACOB,[7] b. Sept. 23, 1822; died March 20, 1826, and was buried at Portsmouth.

v.   MARY EVERT,[7] b. Dec. 25, 1824; died April 29, 1826, and was buried at Portsmouth.

vi.   JACOB,[7] b. July 24, 1826, who removed to Boston, who m. (Oct. 24, 1854) Mary Bertodi Barrett, of that city, resident (1882) in N. York.

vii.   MARY EVERT,[7] b. Aug. 28, 1828, who m. (June 29, 1852) William Hobbs Goodwin, of North Berwick, Me., who removed to Jamaica Plain, Mass., the following year, and now resident there.

viii.   GEORGE BLUNT,[7] b. Jan. 31, 1831, who m. (Feb. 7, 1861) Mary Elizabeth Thompson, of Portsmouth, removed to Quincy, Mass., and who died there, Sept. 25, 1881, leaving issue, and was buried at Portsmouth.

---

daughter of Hon. Jotham Odiorne, of Newcastle. The Hon. *John Rindge* was a merchant of high standing and handsome estate. He served repeated terms in the provincial assembly, was Commissioner to the Court of Great Britain in behalf of the province, to settle the boundary line between New Hampshire and Massachusetts, in 1731–32, while he was of his Majesty's Council in 1738–40.   By his wife Ann Odiorne he had issue of thirteen children, to wit : *Elizabeth,* born July 29, 1717, who m. Mark Hunking Wentworth ; *Isaac,* born 1719 ; George, born 1721 ; *Ann,* born Aug. 20, 1723, who m. Daniel Peirce ; *Mehetabel,* born Sept. 22, 1725, who m. Daniel Rogers ; *John,* born July 23, 1727 ; *Daniel,* born Sept. 18, 1729 ; *Daniel,* born Oct. 5, 1731, who m. Olive Huske ; *William,* born April 21, 1734 ; *Isaac,* born Oct. 20, 1735, who m. Sarah Purr ; *Jotham,* born Feb. 28, 1737, who m. Sarah Vaughan ; *Benjamin,* born May 31, 1739 ; and lastly, *George,* born 1740.

* Mark Rogers, of Portsmouth, tenth child of Hon. Daniel and Mehetabel (Rindge) Rogers.   He was a descendant through *Daniel* of Portsmouth, Rev. *Nathaniel* of Portsmouth, and Rev. *John* of Ipswich, of the Rev. *Nathaniel Rogers,* the first New England ancestor of the family, who emigrated to Ipswich, Mass., in 1636, who was the son of the Rev. John Rogers, of Dedham, co. Essex, England, a renowned Puritan preacher. Inasmuch as the impression has been long prevalent that this well-known divine was a grandson of the famous Marian proto-martyr, it is interesting to note the fact that the closest researches by the late eminent genealogist, Joseph Lemuel Chester, LL.D., himself a descendant of the Rev. John Rogers, of Dedham, have utterly failed to substantiate the claim.   "He has so long been supposed," says Colonel Chester, "to have been a grandson of the Martyr, that, especially in New England, where his descendants are very numerous, it will be deemed little less than heresy when it is said that there is no reasonable ground for supposing that he occupied that relation.   He claims no such ancestry for himself, nor does any one do so for him until the time of Hutchinson, whose history of the Colony of Massachusetts was first published in London about 1760.   That historian, noticing the death of Nathaniel Rogers, the celebrated New England divine, says that 'he was the son of Mr. John Rogers, a celebrated Puritan preacher of Dedham, England, *descended from the Proto-martyr of Queen Mary's reign,*' and quotes Hubbard (History of New England) as his authority for the entire paragraph.   Strangely enough, Hubbard says nothing of the kind, and in no place in his history gives the most distant hint of such a relationship." Col. Chester adds that he is sorry thus to be compelled to destroy the pleasing delusion in which the descendants of John Rogers of Dedham have so long indulged, but that numerous class must console themselves with the reflection that their immediate ancestor was, nevertheless, one of the best and most venerated men of his times.

5

WILL OF JOHANNES' WENDEL, OF ALBANY.

In the Name of God, Amen, the Twenty-third day of November, 1691, in the Third Year of our most Sovereign Lord and Lady, William and Mary, by the Grace of God, of England, Scotland, France and Ireland, King and Queen, I, Johannes' Wendel, of the' City of Albany, Merchant, although weak and sickly in body, yet of good, perfect and sound Memory, praised be Almighty God therefor, do Make and Ordain this my present Will and Testament, in manner and form following ; that is to say :

First, I Commend myself and all my Whole Estate to the Mercy and Protection of Almighty God, being fully Persuaded by His Holy Spirit, through the Death and Passion of Jesus Christ, to obtain full Pardon and Remission of all my sins, and to inherit everlasting life, to which, the Holy Trinity, one coequal Deity, be all Honor and Glory forever, Amen. And Touching such Temporal Estate of Lands, Houses, Goods, Chattels and Debts, as the Lord hath been pleased, (far beyond my Deserts), to Bestow upon me, I do Order, Give, Bequeath and Dispose the same in manner and form following :

Imprimis my Will is that my well-beloved wife, Elizabeth Wendel, shall Have and Keep, Hold and Possess my Whole Estate, both Lands, Houses, Lots, Goods and Chattels, and all my moveables during her Natural Life, out of which she is to Bring up, Educate and Maintain my Eleven Children, vizt: Elsie and Mary Wendel, begotten by my first wife Marytje Jillisse (Meyer), to which two daughters my Wife is to pay as soon as they come to Age, or to be Married, Three Hundred and forty Beavers, and the other moveables due to them for their Mother's Portion, or Inheritance, according to the Instrument made thereof, which I Will shall take its Effect to all Intents and Purposes, and moreover have an Equal Share of my Estate with my Other Children, and also to Bring up, Educate and Maintain my Nine Children begotten by Elizabeth, my Present Wife, called Abraham, Susanna, Catalyntje, Elizabeth, Johaunes, Ephraim, Isaac, Sarah and Jacob Wendel, and such other Children as it shall Please God to send me by her, until they shall severally come of Age, or to be Married, but if my Wife shall happen to re-marry, then my Will is that she give and Exhibit a Perfect Inventory upon Oath of all the Whole Estate, Real and Personal, which is to be apprised by Indifferent and Judicious Men, and Equally Divided,

one Moiety thereof for the Behoof of my said Eleven Children, which half
I Will to be Equally Divided among them, or so many of them as shall then
be alive; and the other Moiety for my said well-beloved Wife, which Portions of my said Children she is to keep until they come to Age or be Married, she giving sufficient Security for the same. **Provided,** Lands and
Houses be also Apprised and Allotted to my Sons, as hereafter is Specified,
they being accountable to the Children what the said Lands shall be Valued
above their Proportion in the Estate, vizt: I do Give and Bequeath to my
Eldest Son Abraham, and to His Heirs forever, all my Seventh Part of
the Land commonly Called *Saraghtogo*, my share being that Farm that lies
to the Southward of the Fish Creek, so called, which separates the land of
Robert Livingston and mine, being Bounded on the South by Dirk Wessel's, with my Proportion of Wood-Land belonging thereunto, alway Provided the same Be Apprised by Indifferent Persons, when he shall come
to Age or be Married, he paying the surplusage what it be more valued
than His Portion with the other Children. I do Give and Bequeath unto
my son Johannes and to his Heirs forever, all my Land commonly Called
Steen Rabie, on the East side of Hudson's River, with all the Houses, Barns,
Yards and other appurtenances, the Island called *Walrisch Island* and that
Belongs to said tract of Land, which is to be Apprised when he comes to
Age, and if the apprisement amounts to more than his Equal Share in my
Estate, he is to pay it to my other Children to make them equal. I do
Give and Bequeath to my Son Ephraim and to His Heirs forever, all my
Part, Share and Portion of the land Called Blenkenburgh, both at the Strand
and upon the Flatts or Plains, which is Also to be Apprised, as the other
Lands above mentioned, and if the apprisement amounts to more than the
Equal Proportion in said Estate, he is to pay it to my other Children, to
make them Equal with him. My Will is further, that if any of the said
Tracts of Land Bequeathed to my Sons aforesaid should happen to be apprised less than their Portion in the Estate, that so much of the Estate be
paid to them as to make it up with the rest of the Children. I do Give unto
my well-beloved Wife, my House which I now live in, situate and being
between the widow of Jacob Glen and Peter Davidtse Schuyler, which is to
be apprised and deducted out of the Moiety of the Estate which she is to
have; and if she remains a Widow, she is to Keep, Hold, Enjoy and Possess the Whole Estate during her Natural Life, and to Give to my said
Children such Portions and Outfitts as she shall see meet when they come
to Age, or to be Married, and after my Wife's decease the Whole Estate,
Real and Personal, to be Equally Divided among my Sons and Daughters,
Excepting that I do give to my Eldest Son, Abraham, the Sum of Three
Pounds current money of this Province, besides his Portion with the Rest
of my Children, wherewith he is to Rest Satisfied of any Pretence that he
might make as my Eldest Son, and share then as the others do, and

whereas I have Ordered my Sons Abraham, Johannes and Ephraim, Lands for their Portion as above is Expressed, if any of the said Sons should happen to Dye before they come to Age, then my Sons Isaac and Jacob are to have the same successively on the said condition.

Lastly, I do Make, Constitute, Ordain and Appoint my dear and well-beloved Wife Sole Executrix of this my Last Will and Testament, who is to have the Administration of my Goods and Chattels as Administratrix, as by the Laws of this Government are Admitted to do. I do Nominate and Appoint my beloved brother-in-law Mr Jacob Staets, and Mr Joh: Lansingh, to be Tutors and Trustees over my said wife and Children, and to Aid and Assist my Wife in the Administration of said Estate.

In Witness whereof, I have Hereunto sett my Hand and Seal, in Albany, at my Dwelling House, the Day and Year first above written.

{ SEAL. }

Signed and Delivered in the Presence of
    Barent Lewis, }
    Gerrit Lansingh. }

[Reprinted, with additions, from the

NEW ENGLAND HISTORICAL AND GENEALOGICAL REGISTER for July, 1882.]

APPENDIX.

[NOTE A.]

THE OCTROY, OR GENERAL CHARTER OF 1614.

[From the *Acte Boek* of the States General in the Royal Archives at the Hague.]

THE STATES GENERAL OF THE UNITED NETHERLANDS: To all who shall see these presents or hear them read, *Greeting:* BE IT KNOWN, Whereas, we understand it would be honorable, serviceable and profitable to this Country, and for the promotion of its prosperity, as well as for the maintenance of seafaring people, that the good Inhabitants should be excited and encouraged to employ and occupy themselves in seeking out and discovering Passages, Havens, Countries and Places that have not before now been discovered nor frequented; and being informed by some Traders that they intend with God's merciful help, by diligence, labor, danger and expense, to employ themselves thereat, as they expect to derive a handsome profit therefrom, if it pleased Us to favor, privilege and charter them, that they alone might resort and sail to and frequent the Passages, Havens, Countries and Places to be by them newly found and discovered, for six voyages as a compensation for their outlays, trouble and risk, with interdiction to all directly or indirectly to resort or sail to, or frequent the said passages, havens, countries or places, before and until the first discoverers and finders thereof shall have completed the aforesaid six voyages:

Therefore, We having duly weighed the aforesaid matter, and finding as hereinbefore stated, the said understanding to be laudable, honorable and serviceable for the prosperity of the United Provinces, and wishing that the experiment be free and open to all and every of the Inhabitants of this country, have invited and do hereby invite, all and every of the Inhabitants of the United Netherlands to the aforesaid search, and therefore, have granted and consented, grant and consent hereby that whosoever any new *Passages, Havens, Countries* or *Places* shall from now henceforward discover, shall alone resort to the same or cause them to be frequented for four voyages, without any other person directly or indirectly sailing, frequenting or resorting from the United Netherlands to the said newly discovered and found passages, havens, countries or places, until the first discoverer shall have made or cause to be made the said four voyages, on pain of confiscation of the goods and ships wherewith the contrary attempt shall be made, and a fine of Fifty Thousand Netherlands Ducats, to the profit of the aforesaid finder or discoverer.

Well understanding that the discoverer, on completion of the first voyage, shall be holden within fourteen days after his return from said voyage, to render unto Us a pertinent Report of the aforesaid discoveries and adventures, in order on hearing thereof, We may adjudge and declare, according to circumstances and distance, within what time the aforesaid four voyages must be completed. Provided that we do not understand to prejudice thereby, or in any way to diminish our former Charters and Concessions: And if one or more Companies find and discover, in or about one time or one year, such new Passages, Countries, Havens or Places, the same shall Conjointly enjoy this Our Grant and Privilege; and in case any differences or questions concerning these or otherwise should arise or occur from this our Concession, the same shall be decided by Us, whereby each shall have to regulate himself. And in order that this Our Concession shall be made known equally to all, We have ordered that these be published and affixed at the usual places in the United Countries.

Thus done at the Assembly of the Lords States General at the Hague, the XXVIIth of March XVI^c and fourteen. Was parapheered.

J. van Oldenbarnevelt ^{vt.}

Under stood—By order of the Lords States General.

(*Signed*) C. Aerssen.

N. Y. Col. Mss. Holland Doc. I.

[Note B.]

THE SPECIAL TRADING LICENSE GRANTED TO THE UNITED NEW NETHERLAND COMPANY.

[From the Minute on half a sheet of paper, in the Royal Archives at the Hague, File *Loopende.*]

The States General of the United Netherlands to all to whom these presents shall come, Greeting: Whereas, *Gerrit Jacobz Witssen,* antient Burgomaster of the City Amsterdam, *Jonas Witssen, Simon Morrissen,* owners of the ship named the *Little Fox,* whereof Jan De With has been Skipper; *Hans Hongers, Paulus Pelgrom, Lambrecht Van Tweenhuyzen,* owners of the two ships named the *Tiger* and the *Fortune,* whereof Aedriaen Block and Henriek Corstiaenssen were Skippers; *Arnolt Van Lybergen, Wessel Schenck, Hans Claessen* and *Berent Sweertssen,* owners of the ship named the *Nightingale,* whereof Thys Volckertssen was Skipper, Merchants of the aforesaid City Amstelredam, and *Pieter Clementssen Brouwer, Jan Clementssen Kies,* and *Cornelis Volekertssen,* Merchants of the City of Hoorn, owners of the ship named the *Fortuyn,* whereof Cornelis Jacobssen Mey was Skipper, all now associated in one Company, have respectfully represented to Us, that they, the petitioners, after great expenses and damages by loss of ships and other dangers, had during the present year, discovered and found with the above named five ships, certain *New Lands* situate in America, between New France and Virginia, the Sea Coasts whereof lie between forty and forty-five degrees of latitude, and now called New Netherland: And whereas We did in the month of March last, for the Promotion and Increase of Commerce, cause to be published a certain General Consent and Charter setting forth that whosoever should thereafter discover new havens, lands, places or passages, might frequent, or cause to be frequented, for four voyages, such newly discovered and found places, passages, havens or lands, to the exclusion of all others from visiting or frequenting the same from the United Netherlands, until the said first discoverers and finders shall, themselves, have completed the said four voyages, or caused the same to be done within the time prescribed for that purpose, under the penalties expressed in the said Octroy, etc, they request that We would accord them due Act of the aforesaid Octroy in the usual form :

Which being considered, We therefore in Our Assembly having heard the pertinent Report of the Petitioners, relative to the discoveries and finding of the said new Countries between the above-named limits and degrees, and also of their adventures, have consented and granted, and by these presents do consent and grant, to the said Petitioners, now united unto One Company, that they shall be privileged exclusively to frequent, or cause to be visited, the above newly discovered lands, situate in America between New France and Virginia, whereof the Sea Coasts lie between the fortieth and forty-fifth degrees of Latitude, now named New Netherland, as can be seen by a Figurative Map hereunto annexed, and that for four Voyages within the term of three years, commencing the first of January, sixteen hundred and fifteen next ensuing, or sooner, without it being permitted to any other person from the United Netherlands to sail to, navigate or frequent the said newly discovered lands, havens or places, either directly or indirectly, within the said three years, on pain of confiscation of the vessel and Cargo wherewith infraction hereof shall be attempted, and a fine of *fifty thousand Netherlands Ducats* for the benefit of said discoverers or finders ; provided nevertheless, that by these presents We do not intend to prejudice or diminish any of our former Grants or Charters ; And it is also Our intention, that if any disputes or differences arise from these Our Concessions, they shall be decided by Ourselves. We therefore expressly command all Governors, Justices, Officers, Magistrates, and Inhabitants of the aforesaid United Countries, that they allow the said Company peaceably and quietly to enjoy the whole benefit of this Our Grant and Consent, ceasing all contradictions and obstacles to the contrary. For such We have found to appertain to the public service.

Given under Our Seal, Paraph and Signature of Our Griffier at the Hague, the XIth of October, 1614.

N. Y. Col. Mss. Holland Doc: I.

[NOTE C.]

THE FIRST INTELLIGENCE RECEIVED BY THE WEST INDIA COMPANY FROM ITS COLONY OF NEW NETHERLAND. PURCHASE OF MANHATTAN ISLAND.

[From the Original in the Royal Archives at the Hague, File *West India*.]

HIGH AND MIGHTY LORDS :

Yesterday arrived here the ship *The Arms of Amsterdam*, which sailed from New Netherland, out of the River Mauritius,* on the 23rd September. They report that our people are in good heart, and live in Peace there ; the Women also have borne some children there.† They have purchased the Island Manhattes from the Indians for the Value of 60 guilders ; 'tis 11,000 morgens in size.‡

* The Dutch name for the Hudson, given in honor of the Prince of Orange.
† The birth of the first white child in the Province, a female, occurred June 9, 1625.
‡ The Rhynland rod was the Dutch measure for land, and contained twelve feet, each foot containing 12.36 inches English. There are five rods to a Dutch chain, and six hundred square Dutch rods constitute a *morgen.—Peter Fauconnier's Survey Book.*

They had all their grain sowed by the middle of May, and reaped by the middle of August. They send thence samples of summer grain ; such as Wheat, Rye, Barley, Oats, Buckwheat, Canary seed, Beans and Flax.

The Cargo of the aforesaid Ship is :

7246 *Beaver Skins.*	36 *Wild Cat Skins.*
178½ *Otter Skins.*	33 *Mincks.*
675 *Otter Skins.*	34 *Rat Skins.*
48 *Minck Skins.*	*Considerable Oak Timber and Hickory.*

Herewith, High and Mighty Lords, be commended to the Mercy of the Almighty.

your High Mightinesses obedient,

(*Signed*)   P. SCHAGEN.

In Amsterdam, the 5th November, Ad 1626.
 Received the 7th November, 1626.

To the High and Mighty Lords, ⎫
My Lords the States General   ⎬
at the Hague :   ⎭

N. Y. Col. Mss. Holland Doc. : I.

[NOTE D.]

PATENT TO KILLIAEN VAN RENSSELAER FOR A TRACT OF LAND ON HUDSON'S RIVER.

[From the Royal Archives at the Hague, File *West Indie.*]

Anno 1630, adi 13th of August.   We, the director and Council of New Netherland, residing on the Island Manhatas and in Fort Amsterdam, under the authority of their High Mightinesses the Lords States General of the United Netherlands and the Incorporated West Indin Company, Chamber of Amsterdam, do hereby acknowledge and declare, that on this day, the date underwritten, before us appeared and presented themselves : *Kottomack, Nawanemit, Albantzeene, Sagiskwa* and *Kanaomaek,* owners and proprietors of their respective parcels of land, extending up the (Hudson's) River, South and North, from said Fort unto a little South of Moeneminnes Castle, to the aforesaid proprietors, belonging jointly and in common, and the aforesaid *Nawanemit's* particular land called *Semesseerse,* lying on the East Bank opposite Castle Island off unto the abovementioned Fort ; Item, from *Petanock,* the Millstream, away North to *Negagonse,* in extent about three miles, and declared freely and advisedly for and on account of certain parcels of cargoes, which they acknowledge to have received in their hands before the execution hereof, and by virtue and bill of sale, to hereby Transport, Convey, and Make over to the Mr Killiaen Van Rensselaer, absent, and for whom, We, ex officio and with due stipulation, accept the same ; namely : the respective parcels of land hereinbefore specified, with the timber, appendencies and dependencies thereof, together with all the action, right and jurisdiction to them the Grantors, conjointly or severally belonging ; constituting and surrogating the said Mr Rensselaer in their stead, state and right, real and actual possession thereof, and at the same time giving him full, absolute and irrevocable power, authority and special command to hold in quiet possession, cultivation, occupancy and use *tanquam actor et procurator in rem suam ac propriam*, the land aforesaid, acquired by said Mᵣ Van Rensselaer, or those who may hereafter acquire his interest; also to dispose of do with and alienate it, as he or others should or might do with his other and own Lands and Domains acquired by good and lawful title, without the grantors therein retaining, reserving or holding any, the smallest part, right, action or authority, whether of property, command or jurisdiction, but rather hereby resisting, and renouncing therefrom forever, for the behoof aforesaid; further promising this their conveyance, and whatever may by virtue thereof be done, not only forever to hold fast and irrevocable, to observe and to fulfil, but also to give security for the surrender of the aforesaid land, *obligans et renuncians a bona fide.*

In Testimony is this Confirmed by our Usual Signature, with the ordinary Seal thereunto appending. Done at the aforesaid Island Manahatas and Fort Amsterdam, on the day and year aforesaid.

     (*Signed*)   PETER MINUIT, *Director.*
         PIETER BYLVELT, JACOB ELBERTSS. WISSINCK,
           JAN JANSSEN BROUWER, SYMON DIRCKSS. POS,
           REYNER HARMENSSEN.

JAN LAMPE, *Sheriff.*   *Council.*
                     There was besides :

This conveyance, written with mine only hand, is, in consequence of the Secretary's absence, executed in my presence, on the thirteenth day of August, XVIᶜ and thirty, as above Signed.

           LENART COLE,
             Deputy Secretary.

After collating with the Original, dated, signed and sealed as above, this copy is found to agree with it.

         In Testimony,
           ADRIAEN LOCK,
             Notaris Publ.

       Amsterdam, the Vᵗʰ September, 1672.

N. Y. Col. Mss. Holland Doc. I.

(NOTE E.)

THE LATE REFORMED PROTESTANT DUTCH CHURCH IN ALBANY.
(Removed 1806.)

The author has condensed the following interesting and curious data relative to the ancient edifice named above, from Munsell's Collections for the History of Albany, and the Church Records.

In 1805 the site of the old church (of which we have given a cut supposed to be correct upon page 13 of this book), was sold to the city for five thousand dollars, and in the spring of 1806 the building was taken down, and the materials used in the construction of a church on Beaver Street. A great deal of interest still attaches to this venerable edifice, and its demolition was viewed with painful emotions by many of the old people, who had been so long accustomed to worship there. The site had been selected for the church just a century and a half previous. The one erected in

6

1643 had before 1656 become inadequate to the accommodation of the community, and it had been determined in the preceding year to erect a new building.   To assist this good work the Patroon and co-directors subscribed 1000 guilders, or $400, and 1500 guilders were appropriated from the fines imposed by the court at Fort Orange.

In the early part of the summer of 1656, Rutger Jacobsen, one of the magistrates, laid the corner stone of the sacred edifice in presence of the authorities, both of the town and colonie.   A temporary pulpit was at first erected for the use of the minister, but the settlers subscribed twenty-five beavers to purchase a more splendid one in Holland.   The Chamber of Amsterdam added seventy-five guilders to this sum, for "the beavers were greatly damaged," and with a view to inspire the congregation with more ardent zeal, presented them the next year (1657) with a bell.   When, in 1715, the original structure was beginning to decay, and the congregation becoming too numerous for its dimensions, the foundations of a new one were laid around it, and the walls carried up and enclosed before the first was taken down, so that the customary services were interrupted only three Sabbaths.   The edifice which had been constructed in this extraordinary manner occupied almost the entire width of the present State Street, and extended partly across Broadway.

Many of the present day recollect the small, square, stone building, with its peaked roof and small windows.   The internal arrangement of this church was in keeping with its external appearance ;   and those of the present day who object to gaudy places of worship would probably be startled with the announcement that it was a gaily painted and a richly ornamented church.   The pulpit was of an octagon form, constructed of dark oak, resembling black walnut, richly varnished and polished, four feet in height and three in diameter.   The ceiling and the front of the gallery were painted sky-blue, and the windows covered with richly colored glass, bearing the insignia of the coat-of-arms of the most influential members of the church.*   The pews on the ground floor, with the exception of three, were for the exclusive use of the female members of the congregation ; and of the reserved three, one was appropriated for the use of the governor, the second for the magistrates and officers, and the third for infirm male members of the congregation.   All the male members, except those for whom special provision was made, were compelled to sit in the gallery.   The women were many of them attended by negro servants, particularly in the winter, when they carried foot-stoves containing coals for the purpose of keeping their feet warm.   As these coals expired, they were renewed from the stoves which heated the church.   The latter were placed on each side of the church, over the side aisles, just beneath and projecting beyond the galleries.   They were elevated about eight feet from the floor, upon four upright posts.

The *koster* (sexton) having finished ringing the bell, standing under the cupola in the middle aisle, wound the end of the rope around a high post standing there for the purpose, and went into the gallery to inspect his fires.   The stoves were approached by climbing over the gallery on each side.   The last sexton was Cornelis Van Schaick.   He is represented as having an exalted idea of the dignity of his calling, and did not allow himself to be jostled by any one who passed him while engaged in ringing the bell, without resenting it.   He always carried a switch of some kind when he passed through the galleries, and cut right and left with it among the boys.   The stove doors were always closed by him with a tremendous bang.   All the aisles but the middle one were narrow.   The men below sat upon elevated benches around the wall, with their hats on, and were accustomed to smoke their pipes during sermon time.   Those who occupied the first tier of seats in the gallery hung their hats upon nails which

---

* Our cut of the Wendell arms, which appears on the tabular chart, accurately represents them as stained upon one of the windows at the east end of the church.

studded the whole front of the galleries, presenting a novelty which was rendered more curious by the variety of their style, color and condition.   The roof was ceiled with boards upon the rafters, from the walls to the cupola.   The entrance was through a porch on the south side, and the entrance to the galleries was made by ascending several steps on the east side of the porch.   In this porch the sexton kept his grave-yard tools, and there seems to have been an interior door for his use, connected with the galleries.

When the church was demolished, very few of the armorial bearings upon its stained windows escaped destruction ; still, a few relics were preserved.   Among these is one of its small windows, also the weather-vane, and one of the bags in which the contributions were taken.   But above all, the old pulpit is still in existence, in the possession of the First Church, and forms a very interesting relic.   It was sent over from Holland in 1656, and continued in the service of the church 150 years.   This pulpit was occupied by a long line of ministers, of whose successive pastorates the following is the best account which we are able to give, down to 1882.   The church now consists of three congregations, of which the oldest is the present First Reformed or North Dutch Church, which still retains the old corporate title of THE REFORMED PROTESTANT DUTCH CHURCH IN THE CITY OF ALBANY.

1642–1649.	Dominie	Johannes Megapolensis.
1652–1683.	"	Gideon Schaats.
1671–1680.	"	Wilhelmus Van Nieuwenhuysen.
1683–1699.	"	Godfredius Dellius.
1695–1700.	"	Johannes Petrus Nucella.
1700–1710.	"	Joh: Lydius.
1710–no pastor	"	Gualterus Dubois, (occasional).
1711– " "	"	Petrus Vas, (occasional).
1712–1738.	"	Petrus Van Driessen.
1733–1744.	"	Cornelis Van Schie.
1746–1759.	"	Theodorus Frielinghuyzen.
1760–1790.	"	Eilardus Westerlo.
1776–1779.	Rev.	John H. Livingston, (occasional).
1787–1804.	"	John Bassett.
1796–1802.	"	John B. Johnson.
1805–1820.	"	John M. Bradford.
1823–1834.	"	John Ludlow.
1835–1839.	"	Thomas E. Vermilye.
1842–1845.	"	Duncan Kennedy.
1856–1862.	"	Ebenezer P. Rogers.
1862–——.	"	Rufus W. Clark.

CALL OF THE DOMINIE JOHANNES MEGAPOLENSIS, FIRST PASTOR OF THE REF. PROT. DUTCH CHURCH OF FORT ORANGE.

Whereas, by the state of the navigation in the East and West Indies, a door is opened through the special providence of God, also in New Netherland, for the preach-ing of the Gospel of Jesus Christ for the Salvation of men, as good fruits have been already witnessed there through God's mercy ; and Whereas, the brethren of the Classis of Amsterdam have been notified that Mr. Killiaen Van Rensselaer hath within the said limits in the North River, as Patroon or Lord, founded a Colonie named Rensselaerswyck, and would fain have the same provided with a good, honest and pure preacher, therefore they have observed and fixed their eyes on the reverend, pious and well-learned Doctor Joannes Megapolensis, junior, a faithful servant of the Gospel of the Lord, in the congregation of Schorel and Berge, under the Classis of

Alkmaar, whom ye have also called, after they had spoken with the said Lord, Killiaen Van Reusselaer, in the same manner as they, with his Honor's approbation, do hereby call him to be sent to New Netherland, there to preach God's word in the said colony, to administer the Holy Sacraments of Baptism and the Lord's Supper; to set an example to the congregation, in a Christian-like manner, by public precept; to ordain Elders and Deacons according to the form of the holy Apostle Paul,(I Timothy III-I.); moreover to keep and govern, with the advice and assistance of the same, God's Congregation in good discipline and order, all according to God's Holy Word, and in conformity with the Government, Confession and Catechism of the Netherland Churches and the Synodal Acts of Dordrecht, subscribed by him to this end, with his own hand, and promised in the presence of God, at his ordination, requesting hereby all and every who shall see and read these, to respect our worthy brother as a lawfully called Minister, and him to esteem by reason of his Office, so that he may perform the duty of the Gospel, to the advancement of God's Holy Name, and the conversion of many poor blind men.   May the Almighty God, who hath called him to this Ministry, and instilled this good zeal in his heart, to proclaim Christ to Christians and Heathens in such distant lands, strengthen him more and more in this his undertaking, enrich him with all sorts of spiritual gifts; and bless overflowingly his faithful labors; and when the Chief Shepherd, Christ Jesus, shall appear, present him with the imperishable Crown of Eternal Glory.   Amen.

Thus given in our Classical Assembly at Amsterdam, this XXII^d day of March, 1642. Signed in the name and in behalf of the whole body.

> WILHELMUS SOMMERUS, *Loco Praesidis.*
> ZLOAHAR SWALMIUS, *Scriba Classis.*
> JONAS ABEELS, *Elder.*

Examined and approved by the Directors of the West India Company, Chamber of Amsterdam, VIth June, 1642.

> (*Signed*)   CHARLES LOOTEN, ELIAS DE RAET.

Records of the Reformed Protestant Dutch Church in the City of Albany.

[NOTE F.]

THE WEST INDIA COMPANY'S COMMISSION TO PETER STUYVESANT.

[From the *West Indic* file in the Royal Archives at the Hague.]

The Commissioners on behalf of the General Incorporated West India Company in the United Netherlands : To all those who shall see these presents or hear them read, *Health :* BE IT KNOWN, Whereas, We have deemed it advisable for the promotion of the affairs of the General Incorporated West India Company, not only to maintain the trade and population of the Coasts of New Netherland and the places situate thereabout, together with the Islands of Curacao, Buenaire, Aruba and their dependencies, hitherto encouraged thither from this Country, but also to endeavor to make new treaties and alliances with foreign princes, and to inflict as much injury as possible on the enemy in his Forts and Strongholds, as well by Sea as by Land; for which purposes it becomes necessary to Appoint a person Director:

We therefore, confiding in the probity and experience of Petrus Stuyvesant, formerly intrusted with our affairs at, and the government of, the aforesaid Island of Curacao, and places thereunto depending, being well pleased with his services there, have Commissioned and Appointed and by these presents do Appoint and Commission the said Petrus Stuyvesant, Director over the aforesaid Countries of New Netherland and the places thereunto adjoining, to administer, with the Council as well now, as hereafter to be Appointed with him, the said office of Director, both by water and land, and in Said Quality to attend carefully to the advancement, promotion and preservation of friendship, alliances, trade and commerce; to direct all matters appertaining to Traffic and War, and to maintain in good order everything there for the service of the United Netherlands and the General West India Company; to establish regularity for the security of the places and forts therein; to administer law and justice, as well civil as criminal; and moreover to perform all that concerns his Office and Duties in Accordance with the Charter, and the general and particular Instructions herewith issued, and to be hereafter given to him, as a good and faithful Director is bound and obliged to do by his Oath taken at the hands of the President of our Assembly; which done, we Order and Command all other officers, common soldiers, together with the inhabitants and natives residing in the aforesaid places as subjects, and all whom it might concern, to acknowledge, respect and obey the said Petrus Stuyvesant as our Director in the Countries and places of New Netherland, and to afford all help, countenance and assistance in the performance of these presents, as We have found the same to be for the advantage of the Company.

Done in our Assembly of the XIX., on behalf of the General Incorporated West India Company, in Amsterdam, this Vth May, 1645.

(*Signed.*)   HENRICUS VAN DER CAPELLE THO RYSSEL vt.

By order of the Same,

GYSBERT RUDOLPHI.

N. Y. Col. Mss. Holland Doc. VI.

[NOTE G.]

MINUTE OF PETER STUYVESANT'S HAVING BEEN SWORN IN AS DIRECTOR OF NEW NETHERLAND.

[From the *West Indie Notulen*, in the Royal Archives at the Hague.]

Resolution of the States General:
Saturday, the 28th July, 1646.

Petrus Stuivesant appeared before the Assembly as Director of New Netherland and Director of Curacao, and some other islands mentioned in his Commission, and took according to a certain formulary, the proper Oath, and amongst other things swore specially that he would conform to his Instruction given him by the Assembly of the West India Company, which Instruction is pursuant to their High Mightinesses' order dated the XXVIth instant, exhibited at their High Mightinesses' Assembly, and a copy thereof enregistered in the *Acte Boek*.

N. Y. Col. Mss. Holland Doc. VI.

[NOTE II.]

AT A MEETING OF THE
COMMANDERS AND Honble COUNCIL OF WAR,
HOLDEN ON THE 19th 7bre 1673.

THE COMMISSION OF THE Honble GOVERNOR GENERAL ANTHONY COLVE, RECORDED THIS DAY BY ORDER OF MESS^{rs} THE COMMANDERS.

[Translated from the *Minutes of Council*, in the Original Dutch Record.]

The Honorable Council of War over a squadron of ships now at anchor in Hudson's River, New Netherland, for and in the Name of their High Mightinesses the States General of the United Netherlands, and His Serene Highness the Prince of Orange.

To all who shall see or hear these, GREETING :

Whereas it is necessary to appoint a fit and able person as Governor-General to hold the supreme command over this conquest of New Netherland, with all its appendencies and dependencies, beginning at Cape Hinlopen, or the south side of Delaware Bay, and fifteen miles more southerly, including said bay and South River, as they were formerly possessed by the Directors of the City of Amsterdam, and after by the English government, in the name and on behalf of the Duke of York; and further from the said Cape Hinlopen along the Great Ocean to the East End of Long Island and Shelter Island, and thence westward to the middle of the Channel called the Sound, to a Town called Greenwich on the main, and so to run landward in northerly; provided that such line shall not come within ten miles of the North River, conformable to the provisional settlement of the boundary made in 1650, and afterwards ratified by the States General, February 23, 1656, and January 23, 1664; with all the Lands, Islands, Rivers, Lakes, Kills, Creeks, Fresh and Salt Waters, Fortresses, Cities, Towns and Plantations therein comprehended.

Wherefore, being sufficiently assured of the capacity of Anthony Colve, Captain of a Company of Dutch Infantry, in the Service of Their High Mightinesses the States-General of the United Netherlands, and His Serene Highness the Prince of Orange, by virtue of our Commission granted us by their before mentioned High Mightinesses and His Serene Highness, we have Appointed, Commissioned and Qualified, and we do by these presents Commission and Qualify the said Captain Anthony Colve to be Governor-General of this Country and Forts thereunto belonging, with all the appendencies and dependencies thereof, to Govern, Rule and Protect them from all Invasions of enemies, as he, to the best of his abilities, shall judge most necessary. We therefore charge all high and low officers, Justices, Magistrates, and other Commanders, Soldiers, Burghers, and all the Inhabitants of this Country, to Acknowledge, Honor, Respect and Obey said Anthony Colve as their Governor-General, for such we have judged necessary for the service of the Country. All subject to the Approbation of our Principals.

Thus done at Fort Willem Hendrik, the 12th day of August, 1673.

(*Signed*)   JACOB BENCKES,
                               CORNELIS EVERTSE, Junr.

N. Y. Col. Mss. XXIII. Office of the Secretary of State.

INDEX.

INDEX.

7

MISCELLANEOUS INDEX.

www.ingramcontent.com/pod-product-compliance
Lightning Source LLC
Chambersburg PA
CBHW030901260626
47169CB00008B/2626